Cast of Characters

Doan, a California private eye. He'd rather do "this, that and the other" with a female companion than help out the feds, but the government persuades him to find an ore deposit important to the war effort. The deposit is located somewhere near Heliotrope, a town on the state line so offensive that neither California nor Nevada will claim it. He's aided in that effort by his partner,

Carstairs, a fawn-colored Great Dane whom Doan had won in a crap game, and who is Doan's superior in every way imaginable. He'd rather Doan not drink and he certainly doesn't want to be around when Doan does the "other." Carstairs isn't impressed by many people but

Susan Sally, a beautiful film star, makes even Carstairs sit up and take notice.

Elmer A. MacAdoo always takes notice of Susan Sally. He's her agent and he collects ten percent of every dollar she makes. She makes a lot of dollars.

Harriet Hathaway is a very patriotic young woman who is on her way to join the WAACs when she meets up with Doan and finds herself shanghaied into his "command."

Mr. Blue tells Harriet he's not in the army because he didn't know there was a war but he wouldn't have signed up had he known. She's sure she can help him see the error of his ways.

Dust-Mouth Haggerty is an old desert rat who knows where the ore can be found, only he figures the government built Boulder Dam just to irritate him and he isn't about to help them.

Doc Gravelmeyer is Heliotrope's only doctor. He's also the coroner and the undertaker. Undertaking is about to become a growth industry in Heliotrope.

Edmund is a hotel room clerk who doesn't care if he bends a few rules since he's planning on quitting soon.

Arne and **Barstow** are the two G-men given the thankless task of keeping tabs on Doan.

Free-Look Jones is either an agent, a private eye or a salesman. Whatever he is, he's not someone you'd turn your back on.

Tonto Charlie was stabbed in the neck by Free-Look just because he cheated at cards.

Peterkin is Heliotrope's sheriff. From time to time he arrests Doan.

Harold runs the local jail and rents out cells at a very reasonable rate.

H. Pocus is an alias sometimes used by Doan. The "H" stands for Hocus. You probably guessed that.

I. Doanwashi is the alias Doan uses when he's masquerading as a Japanese spy.

Books by Norbert Davis

The Carstairs & Doan trilogy
The Mouse in the Mountain (1943)
Sally's in the Alley (1943)
Oh, Murderer Mine (1946)

Murder Picks the Jury (1946)
as by Harrison Hunt,
written in collaboration with
W.T. Ballard

The Adventures of Max Latin (1988)
A Collection of Short Stories

Sally's
in the
Alley

A Carstairs & Doan Mystery

by

Norbert Davis

The Rue Morgue Press
Boulder, Colorado

For
my aunt
Jeanette Harrison, M.D.

Sally's in the Alley
was first published in 1943
New material copyright © 2002
by The Rue Morgue Press

ISBN: 0-915230-46-1

Any resemblance between the characters in this
book and persons living or dead would likely
lead to their inclusion in Ripley's *Believe It Or Not!*

Printed by Johnson Printing
Boulder, Colorado

PRINTED IN THE UNITED STATES OF AMERICA

Norbert Davis

NORBERT DAVIS first introduced us to Doan, his private eye hero, in the 1943 novel *The Mouse in the Mountain* by saying he was "short and a little on the plump side, and he had a chubby, pink face and a smile as innocent and appealing as a baby's. He looked like a very nice, pleasant sort of person, and on rare occasions he was." He sounds like the typical hard-boiled hero of the time, but readers back then were in for a surprise.

That surprise was his partner, a sidekick who bears little resemblance to the other private eye sidekicks of the era, such as Sam Spade's Miles Archer or Nero Wolfe's Archie Goodwin. His full name is Dougal's Laird Carstairs and he boasts a pedigree that puts Doan's to shame. A Great Dane, Carstairs is in a class all to himself in a long and illustrious succession of pets used in crime fiction, although we suspect Carstairs would tear your arm off if you called him a "pet." He certainly views himself as the dominant partner in the Carstairs and Doan Detective Agency, even though Doan "won" him in a crap game. Part of that dominance comes from his sheer size. Carstairs isn't just big. He is enormous. Davis describes him: "Standing on four legs, his back came up to Doan's chest. He never did tricks. He considered them beneath him. But had he ever done one that involved standing on his hind feet, his head would have hit a level far above Doan's. Carstairs was so big he could hardly be called a dog. He was a sort of new species." Doan also figures that Carstairs is his intellectual superior as well as being far better mannered. Boozing offends Carstairs, and Doan's frequent imbibing (from which he never shows any ill effect) always elicits a menacing growl, especially in the second book in the series, *Sally's in the Alley* (1943).

Hard-boiled fiction was supposed to put the emphasis on action, and although you'll find plenty of that in Davis' books, his real forte was comedy. And Davis was at his comic best in the three novels (the third was a 1946 paperback original *Oh, Murderer Mine*) and two short

5

stories ("Cry Murder" and "Holocaust House") that showcased Doan and his remarkable sidekick. Modern private eye writer Bill Pronzini said Davis "was one of the few writers to successfully blend the so-called hard-boiled story with farcical humor."

While the Doan and Carstairs canon make up three of only four books Davis published in his lifetime, he was an extremely prolific writer of short stories, although writing wasn't his first choice as a career. Born on April 18, 1909, in Morrison, Illinois, Davis moved with his family to California in the late 1920s, where he attended college, eventually earning a law degree from Stanford although he never bothered to take the bar exam. By the time he graduated he was an established pulp magazine writer. His stories were appearing in the leading pulps of the day, including *Dime Detective*, *Double Detective*, and *Detective Fiction Weekly* as well as *Black Mask*. Nor did he confine himself to crime fiction. He wrote whatever he could sell—adventure stories, love stories, westerns. In fact, one western story, "A Gunsmoke Case for Major Cain," was filmed in 1941 as *Hands Across the Rockies*, starring B western actor Wild Bill Elliot.

In his early years as a pulp writer, Davis was married to his first wife, Frances, and lived in Los Altos in the San Francisco Bay Area. After divorcing Frances, he married another writer, Nancy Kirkwood Crane, whose stories were appearing in such higher-paying slick magazines as *The Saturday Evening Post*. Davis himself began to make the switch from the pulps to the slicks in the mid-forties, selling a number of humorous short stories to them but never experiencing total success in this new medium. By the late 1940s, his stories were being rejected by some of the slicks while his wife's career was progressing at a rapid rate. In 1949, he and Nancy moved from California to Salisbury, Connecticut, perhaps to be closer to the New York publishing houses. That same summer, Davis drove to the resort community of Harwick, Massachusetts, on Cape Cod. There, early in the morning of July 28, he ran a hose from his car's exhaust to the bathroom of the house where he was staying. His body was discovered there later that day. He was just forty years old. He left no note. At probate, his estate was valued at less than five hundred dollars.

For more information on Davis see Tom & Enid Schantz' introduction to The Rue Morgue Press edition of *The Mouse in the Mountain,* published in 2001.

Chapter One

THIS WILL PROBABLY STRIKE YOU AS HIGHLY improbable if you know your Hollywood, but the lobby of the Orna Apartment Hotel, off Rossmore south of Melrose, is done in very nice taste. It is neat and narrow and dignified, with a conservative blue carpet on the floor and a small black reception desk on a line straight back from the unadorned plate glass door.

At this particular moment its only occupant was the desk clerk. He was small and very young-looking, and he had dark curly hair and a snub nose with freckles across the bridge. His blue eyes were staring with a look of fierce, crosshatched concentration at the pictured diagram of a radio hookup he had spread out on the desk.

The plate glass door opened, and a man came into the lobby with a quietly purposeful air. He was blond and a little better than medium height, and he was wearing an inconspicuous blue business suit. He looked so much like an attorney or an accountant or the better class of insurance broker that it was perfectly obvious what he really was.

He walked up to the desk and said, "Have you a party by the name of Pocus staying here?"

The desk clerk was following the whirligig line that indicated a coil on his diagram with the point of a well-chewed pencil. The pencil point hesitated for a split second and then moved on again.

"No," he said. He didn't have to bother about being courteous because he intended to quit the apartment hotel any minute now and get a job at a fabulous salary in a war plant installing radios in fighter planes.

The blond man took a leather folder from his pocket, opened it, and spread it out on the radio diagram. "Take a look at this."

7

The clerk studied the big gold badge for a second and then looked up slowly. "You're a G-man."

The blond man winced slightly. "I'm a special agent of the Department of Justice. Let's start over again. What's your name?"

"Edmund."

"All right, Edmund. Have you got a party by the name of Pocus staying here? H. Pocus or Hocus Pocus?"

"No," said Edmund. He cleared his throat. "Will you excuse me for a second? I've got to call and wake up one of our tenants. He works on the swing shift, and he has to get waked up and eat before—"

The blond man punched him suddenly and expertly in the chest with a stiffened forefinger. "Get away from the switchboard. You're not tipping anybody off." He whistled shrilly through his teeth.

Another man came in the front door. He was short and stocky, and he had sleepy brown eyes and a scar on his nose. A third man came in from the hall that led to the back door. He was very tall and thin, stooped a little. He wore a light topcoat, and he kept his hands in its pockets.

"They're here," said the blond man. "Come on, Edmund. Give. Which apartment are they in?"

Edmund stood mute.

The blond man watched him curiously. "Are you scared of them?"

"Yes," said Edmund.

"Listen, son," said the blond man. "This is the government you're talking to now. If either one of them even made a pass at you, we'd put them away in Alcatraz."

"How do I know they'd stay there?" Edmund asked.

"All right," said the blond man. "Come on out from behind that desk. Sit down in that chair and rest your feet. Look up the tenant index, Curtis."

The stocky man went behind the desk, found the file of register cards, and ran through them expertly.

"In two-two-nine," he said. He looked under the desk. "Here's the pass key." He flipped it to the blond man.

"Okay," said the blond man. "Stay here and watch the board, Curtis. If anybody comes down the elevator, they wait in the lobby. If anyone comes in the front, they wait, too."

"Sure," said Curtis.

"You come with me, Barstow," the blond man said. "We'll take the stairs. Go easy."

They went up to the second floor and along a hall that was carpeted in the same dark blue as the lobby, and stopped in front of the door numbered 229. The blond man fitted the passkey in the lock and turned it without making the slightest sound. He opened the door just as silently.

It was a single apartment, and the big combination living room-bedroom was bright and cheery with the sun coming in a warm, slatted flood through the venetian blinds. There was no one in sight, but a door to the left was slightly open and through it came the pleasantly languid gurgle and splash of bathwater.

The blond man and his tall companion came into the apartment and shut the front door. The blond man nodded meaningly and then, with the tall man close behind him, walked over and opened the bathroom door.

It was a big bathroom and a beautiful one, tastefully decorated now with fat little coils of steam that clung cozily against the ceiling. It was equipped with an outsize sunken tub, and Doan was sitting in it with his back to the door. He was chubby and pink and glistening, and he looked even more innocent and harmless than he usually did. He held a big sponge up over his head and squeezed it and made happy sputtering noises through the resultant flood.

"Now that you're here," he said amiably, "would you mind telling me if I've gotten all the soap off my back?"

"Yes, you have," said the blond man. "How did you know we were here?"

"There's a draft when the front door opens," Doan answered. He turned around in the tub to peer up at them. "Well! The government, no less. I'm honored."

"Yes," said the blond man. "I'm Arne. Department of Justice. This is Barstow. Where's Carstairs?"

"Well," said Doan, "if there should be a fire and you should try to get out of here in a hurry, you'd probably run across him en route."

Barstow turned around with a jerk to look behind him. "Uh!" he said, startled.

Carstairs was standing in the doorway, watching him with narrowed, greenish eyes. Carstairs was a fawn-colored Great Dane about as big as a medium-sized Shetland pony, only Shetland ponies at least make a try at looking amiable most of the time and Carstairs never did. He looked mean. Probably because he was. He had many responsibilities and problems to shorten his temper. Carstairs was so big that the first sight of him was liable to be a considerable shock. It was as though something had suddenly gone wrong with your perspective.

"Relax, stupid," Doan ordered. "These are friends—I hope. At least, if they aren't we can't do much about it."

Carstairs watched him for a second and then turned and disappeared from the doorway.

"Wow!" said Barstow. "I'd heard he was a whopper, but I certainly didn't expect anything like that."

"People rarely do," Doan said. He reached over and turned the drain lever. "Hand me that towel, will you?"

Arne handed him the towel. "You were notified to come in and report to us. Why didn't you do it?"

"I was just getting around to it," Doan said. "Hand me that robe, please."

Arne looked in both pockets of the white robe and then gave it to him. "You didn't get around quick enough, so we did."

"It was nice of you," said Doan. "Let's go out and sit where it's comfortable."

They went out into the living room, and Doan lay down with a luxurious sigh on the blue chesterfield that was pushed in slantwise against the corner.

"Have a chair," he invited. "I'd offer you a drink only Carstairs doesn't approve of it, and he's mad enough at me as it is."

"Where is he?" Barstow asked.

"Behind the chesterfield in the corner where he was when you came in. He's sulking."

"What's he mad at?" Barstow inquired curiously.

"He had to sleep down cellar last night. That offends his dignity."

"Where does he usually sleep?"

"There are twin pull-down beds behind that door," Doan said. "He sleeps in one. I sleep in the other."

"Why didn't he sleep in it last night?"

"Well, it was like this," said Doan. "I had a friend calling on me. She's a very nice girl."

There was a rumbling mumble from behind the chesterfield.

"She is, too!" Doan said indignantly. "Just because she works in a dime store and chews gum is no reason for you to get so huffy about her, you snob. Anyway, we were sitting here doing this, that, and the other, and she said she positively was not going to do the other any more with Carstairs sneering at her while she did it. So I ran him down cellar. Hey, you. Come up for air."

Carstairs' head appeared slowly from behind the chesterfield. He rested his chin on the top of it and looked Doan in the eye without any signs of approval at all.

"Now, look," said Doan. "I've had enough temperament for today. I said I was sorry you had to sleep in the cellar. I apologized."

Carstairs sighed deeply and wearily.

"And I said I'd buy you a steak to make it up to you," Doan told him. "A steak. Get it? Slaver-slaver, mumble-mumble, crunch-crunch. Steak. Now come out from behind there and act civilized."

Carstairs jumped from a sitting position without any visible effort. It was a heart-stopping performance. He sailed clear over the chesterfield and Doan, landing hard enough to rattle the window panes. He licked his chops delicately and politely with a long, red tongue.

"Yes," said Doan. "I said, steak. But not right now. Wait until I finish my business with these gentlemen. In the meantime, lie down before somebody knocks you down."

Carstairs sprawled out on the floor and rolled over on his side with a resigned snort.

Doan nodded at Arne and Barstow. "Well, what can I do for you?"

"You're not a private detective any more," Arne told him.

"Oh, yes," said Doan.

"No. You don't work for the Severn International Detectives now."

"Yes, I do," said Doan. "They don't dare fire me. If I started to talk about that outfit, they'd be bankrupt in five minutes and on their way to jail in ten—if they weren't lynched first."

"Maybe. But anyway, they've loaned you to the government temporarily."

"No," said Doan.

Arne took a letter from his pocket and opened it. "Read this."

Doan read the letter. He came to the signature, and his eyes widened slowly. He read the letter again, and then he folded it up very carefully and handed it back to Arne.

"If you want to call Washington at your expense, you can verify the signature," Arne said.

Doan shook his head. "That won't be necessary. So I'm loaned to the government. All right. What does that make me?"

"A Japanese," Arne said.

"Oh, I don't think the Japs would go for that," Doan told him. "My eyes don't slant enough."

"Not a Japanese national," Arne explained. "A Jap agent."

"A spy!" Doan chortled, pleased. "Now that's something like it! I've always wanted to be a spy. Does it pay well?"

"To you, it pays nothing," Arne informed him. "You're donating your services."

"Oh," said Doan glumly. "What services?"

"You are to go to the Mojave Desert and find a man named Dust-Mouth Haggerty and buy from him the secret of the location of an ore deposit."

"What kind of ore?" Doan asked.

"You wouldn't know if I told you, and besides it's none of your business. Dust-Mouth will know what you're after. Don't pretend to be a mining expert. Tell him you're the forerunner of a Japanese invasion force, sent ahead to locate this deposit so they can take it over when they come and use what they get out of it to blow Washington off the map. Understand that?"

"Yes," said Doan. "But if you don't mind me saying so, it sounds a little on the screwy side from where I sit."

"That's how we want it to sound."

"Oh," said Doan. "I take it that this Dust-Mouth Haggerty doesn't like Washington?"

"Not even any at all," Arne confirmed.

"Why not? That is, providing you admit that you need a reason."

"Have you ever heard of Boulder Dam?"

"Sure."

"That's why. Dust-Mouth claims it was built as part of a conspiracy to defraud him."

"Was it?" Doan asked.

"You'd better practice up thinking so if you're going to negotiate with Dust-Mouth. He had a gold claim on the Colorado River. He was washing out about thirty cents in gold a day. After Boulder Dam was built the river backed up over his claim so that now he can't get at it. He says that was the real reason the dam was built, just to destroy his claim."

"It seems like the long way around," Doan commented.

"Not to Dust-Mouth. His claim was investigated, and he was offered compensation for it, but he wouldn't accept. He says the thirty cents a day was merely the forerunner. He says he was just about to uncover the greatest gold deposit the world has ever seen, such an immense quantity of gold that it would have made him financial emperor of the United States, disturbed the world's balance of trade, and resulted in international crises by the dozen. He says the politicians in Washington built the dam to prevent him from doing that."

"When did he get out?" Doan inquired.

"Of where?"

"Of the insane asylum."

"Six months ago. Don't get the idea that he's a complete whack. He's not. He's a monomaniac. He's hipped on this one point. Other than that, he's pretty shrewd and sometimes nasty. He's just got a mad on with Washington, and he really means it. We've come at him from every direction, but he can spot a government man for a mile, and all he does is froth at the mouth."

"Hmmm," said Doan. "This ore I'm on the hunt for doesn't have anything to do with his gold claim, does it?"

"No. Dust-Mouth is an old-time desert rat. He's been prowling around in the Mojave for forty years. He came across the ore deposit we want on one of his trips. He never filed a claim on it, because the stuff was worth nothing at that time. It is now. In relation to the war effort, it's worth just about any amount you want to name. You'll probably have to promise to pay him a billion dollars for the location."

"What happens if I do, and he shows me where the stuff is, and then I don't pay off?"

Arne shrugged. "That's your problem."

"Yeah," said Doan sourly. "How about giving me some counterfeit money to pay him off with? You've got plenty of that around, haven't you?"

"Yes," Arne said. "But we're not so foolish as to trust you with any of it. You just talk your way out. All we're interested in is the location of that ore deposit."

"Huh," said Doan. "How do I find this guy, Dust-Mouth? The Mojave is a big place."

"Start at a town called Heliotrope."

"Where's that?"

"Either in California or Nevada."

"You said either?" Doan asked.

"Yes. The State of California is now suing the State of Nevada in the Supreme Court to compel Nevada to annex it. Nevada has started a countersuit to compel California to annex it."

"What's the matter with the place?"

"Just everything. Offhand, I can't think of any crime that isn't committed there regularly. You'll feel right at home."

"People circulate more nasty rumors about me," Doan said mildly.

"We don't deal in rumors," Arne said. "Only facts."

"Oh," said Doan.

Arne nodded at him. "Don't cut any corners in front of us. We've got quite a file on you and this hound of yours. There's a car parked in front, downstairs. Use it. In the dash compartment you'll find strip maps with the route to Heliotrope marked on them and an emergency gas rationing book made out in your name."

"What kind of a car?" Doan asked. "Carstairs is particular what he rides in."

"It's a Cadillac."

"Whee!" said Doan. "A new one, I hope, shined up all pretty?"

"Yes. And don't try to mortgage it or sell it because it's government property. Also, don't stall around giving joyrides to people who work in dime stores. Get started for Heliotrope right away"

"Like a flash," said Doan. "How will I get hold of you if I locate the ore deposit?"

Arne stood up. "We'll get hold of you. We can do that very easily, any time. Remember it. Come on, Barstow."

Barstow paused in the doorway and nodded at Doan. "Good luck."

"Well, thanks," said Doan, pleased.

"You'll need it," said Barstow, closing the door softly.

Doan got up off the chesterfield and kicked Carstairs in the stomach. "Stop snoring, and act a little more alert. We are starting on a secret government mission of enormous and far-reaching importance"

Carstairs raised his head and looked at Doan and licked his lips slowly and meaningly.

"Stop nagging!" Doan ordered. "I'm working on that steak right now. Give me time, will you?"

Carstairs let his head fall back on the rug with a disgusted thud.

Chapter Two

DOAN PACKED IN TEN MINUTES FLAT, AND WHEN he got through the apartment looked as though he had done just that, but he didn't. He looked neat and fresh and cool in a light gray suit and a lighter gray hat and gray suede oxfords. He parked his two big, battered suitcases at the door, and as a last move pulled the cushions off the chesterfield and unearthed a Colt Police Positive revolver.

He slid that inside the waistband of his trousers, hooking it in a cloth loop sewn there for that purpose, and then he went over and pulled up the rug in the corner behind the bridge lamp. He found a .25 caliber automatic hidden there. He put that in the breast pocket of his coat and pushed an ornamental dark blue handkerchief down on top of it to keep it in place.

He was all ready to go when he had another thought. He took out his wallet and counted the money in it. The sum did not impress him. He put the wallet away and picked up the telephone from its stand beside the chesterfield.

The line clicked, and then a voice said cautiously

"Yes?"

"Is this Edmund, you rat?" Doan snarled. "I'll have something to say to you in a minute, but right now you connect me with the manager! I've got a beef with him!"

"This—this is the manager, Mr. Pocus."

"Oh, it is, is it? Well, what do you mean by tipping me off to those government men? Do you want to get me hung or something? You squealer! You doublecrosser! Do you think I'm going to recommend this joint to any of my pals as a hideout if that's the way you're going to act?"

"Wha-wha-what?"

"Don't try that innocent stuff! I'm going to come down there and tear you up in little pieces! Just listen!"

Doan kicked Carstairs again and then leaned down and held the telephone close to his face. "Give," he whispered.

Carstairs snarled into the receiver. He looked enormously bored while he was doing it, but over the telephone the sound must have been horrible, because Carstairs had a company snarl that began low and ended high and undulated blood-chillingly in the middle register.

"There!" said Doan into the telephone. "Did you hear that? That's just a sample of what you're going to get when . . ." He listened and then said in a milder inquiring tone, "Hello? Hello, Mr. Rogan? Are you there?"

There was no answer.

Doan put the telephone back on its stand, took hold of Carstairs' spiked collar and heaved. "Come on. Hurry up."

Carstairs got up one foot at a time and sauntered to the door. Doan opened it for him and picked up the suitcases and bunted Carstairs in the rear with one of them.

"Go on. Get moving."

They went down the hall and down the stairs into the lobby. There was not a soul in sight.

Doan put his bags down and hammered vigorously on the desk. "Service! Service here! Mr. Rogan! Edmund!"

No one answered. No one appeared.

"Now imagine that," Doan said to Carstairs. "Obviously I can't be expected to pay my bill if thereisn't anyone to pay it to, can I? The answer is no. So I won't pay. That will be a lesson to them to give more attention to their business in the future."

He picked up the suitcases again and negotiated them and Carstairs through the plate glass door.There was a black sedan glittering with chrome and a beautifully high, lustrous polish parked at the curb.

"Ah-ha!" said Doan. He opened one of the rear doors and heaved the bags inside and then walked all around the car twice, rubbing his hands blissfully. "Take a squint at this, kid. We're coming up in the world . . . Carstairs! Where are you?"

There was a slight typhoon taking place in the thick, neatly trimmed shrubbery that marched precisely along the front of the apartment building. Shrubs heaved back and forth wildly, and branches crackled.

"Carstairs!" Doan shouted. "Oh, you would pick atime like this! Rogan is going to get over being scared and call copper on us or something if we don't get out of here. Hurry up!"

Carstairs' head appeared out of the greenery. He did not look like he was hurrying or even intended to.He blinked at Doan in a fatuous and pleased way.Doan started for him. Carstairs sighed comfortably and came out of the bushes. Doan got him by the collar and dragged him across the walk to the open rear door of the Cadillac.

"Get in there!"

He heaved vigorously, and Carstairs allowed himself to be urged through the door. Doan slammed it with a thump and crawled into the front seat. He started the car and drove off down the street with a viciously triumphant clashing of gears.

He drove over to Rossmore and up Rossmore to where it turns into Vine, and up Vine to Sunset Boulevard. He swung around to the right on Sunset, narrowly missing twenty-five sailors, sixteen soldiers and two marines who were doing sentry duty on the corner in the hopes of seeing a movie star. He drove two blocks farther and pulled up in front of an open air market.

It was really quite a marvelous place. It covered an area half the size of a city block, and you could buy anything in it from lollipops to life insurance. Doan got out of the car and headed for the long and empty meat counter. There was only one butcher behind it, and he looked as though he wished he were somewhere else.

"I'd like a three-pound porterhouse steak," Doan told him.

"So would I," said the butcher.

"I know you've got one hidden out in the icebox," Doan said.

"How do you know?" the butcher asked.

"I'm a Japanese spy. We spies get around."

"Palooey," said the butcher in a disgusted tone. "Now it's jokes I have to put up with. In my financial condition. All right. So suppose I've got a steak in the icebox. So why should I give it to you?"

"That's my car out in front—the big, shiny one. Take a look at what's in the back seat."

The butcher said: "I wouldn't care if..." He paused for a long moment. "Just what is that?"

"A dog."

"It's got awful big teeth for a dog," the butcher said slowly. "And I don't know as I like the way he's lookin' at me."

"The teeth are bigger at closer range," Doan said. "Would you like a demonstration?"

"No," said the butcher quickly. "Now listen, chum. I don't want no trouble with you or that gargoyle, but I can't sell you that steak. It was ordered three weeks ago by an old customer of mine. She's a very, very special customer. She's Susan Sally, the movie gal."

"She doesn't need a steak. She's too fat now."

"Fat?" the butcher echoed, stunned. "Susan Sally? Say listen, she comes in here all the time in nothing but shorts and a bandanna. I mean, short shorts and a bandanna the size of a cocktail napkin. She ain't fat."

"She will be if she eats too many steaks. You wouldn't want that to happen, would you?"

"I should say not," said the butcher.

"Give me the steak and save the risk. Look at my car now."

"Hey!" said the butcher, alarmed. "He can't get through that window, can he?"

"He probably could if I called to him. Shall I? The only trouble is that I can't control him. He runs around snapping and gnashing, and he's awfully careless about what he gnashes on."

"You're threatening me," said the butcher. "That's what you're doing."

"I'm glad you finally found it out. Are you going to give me a steak out of the icebox or off of you?"

"It's a hell of a fine thing, that's all I got to say. A man can't even do business any more without being submitted to terrorism."

The butcher went stamping down the counter and opened the heavy icebox door and went inside. He came out again carrying a big, rich red steak reverently in front of him. He plopped it down on the scales, and the dial swung just short of the three-pound mark.

"Okay," said Doan. "Now put it through the grinder."

"Grinder!" the butcher repeated, horrified. "This steak? This steak here?"

"Yes."

"Oh-oh," the butcher mumbled. He ran the steak through the grinder, turning his head away to keep from witnessing its desecration. He wrapped up the results in oiled paper and slapped it on the counter.

"There! Now I hope you're happy!"

"Sure," said Doan. "I see you've got your ceiling prices pasted up over there."

"Yeah. And we follow 'em, too."

"That's fine. I notice that the ceiling price on dog meat is twelve cents a pound. This wasn't quite three pounds, but I'll be generous about it. Here's thirty-six cents and a penny for tax, and you won't need my rationing book because dog meat and scraps don't come under the rules."

The butcher's face was very pale. "Chum," he whispered, "you can't do this to me."

"Thanks," said Doan. "Good-by." He headed for the car.

The butcher leaned over the counter and pointed a long, accusing arm. "Oh, you wait! If you ever meet up with Susan Sally . . . And I'm gonna tell her you said she was fat! You're gonna be a sad man if she ever lays hold of you!"

Doan ignored him. He got in the car and let Carstairs sniff the meat and then drove down Sunset until he located an open-air, car-service restaurant. He drove the Cadillac in under the wooden, pagodalike awning and parked. Grunting and groaning with the effort, he leaned over the back of the seat and opened one of his bags and took out a square cardboard carton.

A very trim and trig little girl in red pants and a red jacket and a high bussar's hat with a red plume on it came up and slapped a card on the windshield and leaned in the window, all glistening teeth and lipstick and beaded eyelashes.

"Good afternoon, sir! And what will—" Her smile went away and left her face as blank as a freshly whitewashed wall. "What's that in the back seat?"

"Just a dog," Doan said. "A poor, harmless, little puppy that loves women and children."

"He looks awful—hungry."

"That's because he is. And speaking of that . . ."

Doan unwrapped the meat and held it up for her to see, rich and luscious in its nest of pink oiled paper.

"Gee!" said the waitress. "Meat!"

"Right," Doan agreed complacently. "Now I'll tell you what I want you to do with it. Take it into your kitchen and put it in a pan and put the pan in the oven. Warm the meat. Don't cook it or sear it. Just warm it. Then take it out and put it in a big bowl—a clean one. Follow me?"

The waitress nodded doubtfully. "Yes."

Doan held up the cardboard carton. "Know what these are?"

She nodded again. "Sure. Those are special-extra-fancy English tea biscuits. I've seen them in some of the real high-priced markets in Beverly Hills."

"Okay. After you get the meat warm, take the biscuits out of the box, crumple them carefully, and stir them into the meat. Mix them up nice and smoothly. Got it?"

The waitress had backed a step away from the window. "Yes," she said warily.

Doan took a small green bottle from his pocket. "When you get through mixing the biscuits, pour three drops of this in the bowl and mix that in, too. It's concentrated cod liver oil. Bring a door tray back when you come. Carstairs refuses to eat off the floor. He knows it makes him look like a giraffe taking a drink."

"Is this for the dog?" the waitress asked incredulously.

"Sure."

"Oh!" she gasped, relieved. "I thought it was for you!"

"I wish it was," said Doan. "But if I tried to eat it, you'd hear an awful lot of hell-raising around here. You haven't got anything in the meat line you could put in a sandwich for me, have you?"

"Oh, no."

"Okay. Bring me six melted cheese sandwiches with chopped nuts spread on them and a quart of beer and three glasses of water."

"A quart of beer and three glasses of water?" the waitress repeated.

"Yes."

She shrugged. "It's your plumbing, mister."

She sauntered back into the restaurant. Doan explored in the dashboard compartment and found the strip maps and the gas rationing book Arne had said would be there. He studied his route to Heliotrope, muttering to himself as he calculated mileages.

The waitress reappeared, loaded down with trays. Doan ran down one of the back windows, and she slid one tray inside and fastened it to the door. She clamped the other one over the steering wheel and then made another trip and returned with sandwiches, water, and beer on one arm and a shiny earthenware bowl under the other.

Carstairs mumbled happily at her as she put the bowl on his tray. She gave Doan the beer and the water and the sandwiches and stood watching for a moment, shaking her head slightly, and then went away.

Carstairs was too well-bred to slobber or slop things around, but he ate with a sort of deadly efficiency. Doan was only on his second sandwich when Carstairs began to snuffle commandingly behind his right ear.

Doan picked up the water glasses one after the other and, leaning over the seat-back, poured them into the earthenware bowl which was now as clean and glistening and empty as it had been when it came from the store.

Carstairs slapped his tongue happily in the water and then said: "Whumpf," in a moistly satisfied way. The car rocked back on its springs as he hurled himself full length on the rear seat. He began to snore instantly.

When he had finished his sandwiches, Doan beeped the horn softly, and the waitress came back. She looked at the empty beer bottle and the three empty water glasses and then said:

"It's right over there."

"Thanks," Doan said. "But not now."

"You'll be sorry," said the waitress. "Listen, did you know your back trunk compartment isn't locked? The handle is turned wrong. Somebody's liable to steal your spare if you don't watch out."

"I don't care," Doan told her.

She stared at him. "You don't care if somebody swipes your spare?"

"No. I can easily get another."

"Are you one of these ration bootleggers?"

"No," said Doan. "I'm a Japanese spy. Rationing doesn't apply to spies. Look it up if you don't believe me"

"Huh!" said the waitress. "I'm going to die laughing some day at the funny cracks I hear on this ,job."

"How would you like to go for a ride?" Doan asked. "Up around the hills, and look at the city and stuff."

"The stuff is what I wouldn't go for," she said.

"You'd like me if you knew me better," Doan told her.

"I doubt that, but we'll never find out, will we?"

"Are you married?" Doan inquired.

"Yes."

"Oh, that's a shame," Doan said. "But then we all make mistakes. Why don't you get a divorce? You can get one cheap in Nevada. I'm on my way up that way to do some spying. Come on along. I'll split the expenses with you."

"I can hardly resist, but I think I will. Here's your bottle of cod liver oil. Your bill is a dollar and fifty-three cents"

Doan counted out a dollar and sixty cents. "You gave us such nice service that I'm going to let you keep the change, all for yourself."

"You're too good to me," said the waitress. "Come back again— three weeks after never."

"It's a date," said Doan.

Chapter 3

THE MOJAVE DESERT AT SUNSET LOOKS remarkably like a painting of a sunset on the Mojave Desert which, when you come to think of it, is really quite surprising. Except that the real article doesn't show such good color sense as the average painting does. Yellows and purples and reds and various other violent subunits of the spectrum are splashed all over the sky, in a monumental exhibition of bad taste. They keep moving and blurring and changing around, like the color movies they show in insane asylums to keep the idiots quiet.

After this gaudy display is over the shadows move in, swift and blue and silent, and then the place resembles a rundown graveyard slightly haunted by rattlesnakes and battered beer cans. It is quite un-canny.

The highway that Arne had marked in red on the maps swooped and curved and coiled casually through draws, canyons, barrancas and such other natural barriers as cluttered up the landscape, and Doan drove along it in sort of a mild coma. The sun had rippled the highway sur-face just enough to give the car a sleepy, rocking motion that was very pleasant. Doan was driving at exactly thirty-five miles an hour. Not entirely from choice. Someone had installed a governor on the Cadil-lac. It wouldn't go any faster.

Doan and Carstairs and the Cadillac were all alone and had been for the last two hours. There hadn't been any signs of civilization at all, not even an abandoned gas station. No other cars had passed him going in either direction. It was as though the highway had decided to run off somewhere at random on an errand of its own.

Doan saw the figure when it was almost a mile ahead of him, standing beside the road with the shadows pooling deep around its feet. It looked like a totem pole sawed off at top and bottom, and then as he rolled closer it moved and jiggled its arm, semaphore fashion, and became human.

Doan slowed up. The desert at dusk is not a one hundred percent safe place to pick up hitchhikers. Quite often they rap you on the head and throw you in a ditch where, after suitable curing, your skull makes a nice nesting place for scorpions. However, the prospect didn't bother Doan much. He knew from some spectacular experiences in that line that he was difficult to murder.

The figure, on closer inspection, turned out to be a female one complete in all its component parts and encased in a neat blue slack suit and possessing blond hair done up precisely in a blue snood. It was a young female figure and had an air of coordinated and trained determination.

Doan pulled up beside her. She opened the door opposite him before he had a chance to, and leaned in the car and looked at him. Her features were even and assembled with good taste, and she had earnest, deep blue eyes.

"Hello," said Doan mildly. "Would you like a ride?"

"What's your name?"

"Doan," said Doan.

"I'm Harriet Hathaway, and I'm on my way to Fort Des Moines to join the WAACs and serve my country."

"Happy to meet you," said Doan. "Would you like a ride?"

"Do you propose to make improper advances to me, Mr. Doan?"

"Well, I hadn't thought of it," Doan told her. "But if you really insist I can probably turn up something in that line."

"I don't insist! And if you have any such ideas I advise you to discard them."

"Plunk," said Doan. "Gurgle-gurgle. They're discarded. Would you like a ride?"

"Yes, I would. Don't bother to move, please. I can handle this." She picked up a small, dark blue bag and placed it precisely in the middle of the front seat. She got in and sat on the far side of it and closed the door efficiently. "I'm ready."

Doan started the car.

"If you'd use the clutch properly the gears wouldn't grate that way," Harriet Hathaway informed him. '

"No doubt you're right," said Doan.

"Men are very nasty beasts."

"Aren't they, though?"

"I've just gone through a singularly unpleasant experience with one."

"A fate worse than death?" Doan asked.

"What? No! I'm quite capable of protecting myself from anything like that. I'm the woman's golf champion of Talamedas County."

"Oh," said Doan.

"I was also the runner-up in the finals of the Basin City National Tennis Tourney last year."

"Oh," said Doan.

"I'm also considered the best horsewoman in the Rio Hondo Riding Club."

"Oh," said Doan.

"This experience had nothing whatsoever to do with—with sex."

"It must have been rather dull," Doan observed.

"It was not! It was beastly! This person offered me a ride in Masterville. He was wearing dark glasses and I detest people with weak vision, but I accepted. I was willing to accept any means of transportation to get to my post of duty as rapidly as possible."

"Sure," said Doan. "Through rain and snow the postman always rings twice."

"What?" said Harriet Hathaway. She watched him narrowly for a moment. "Are you intoxicated?"

"Just slightly dizzy," Doan answered.

"It's probably because the sun has been so bright today. You should pull your windshield visor down when it glares. That's what it's for. But to go back to this horrible person who gave me the ride. He was a slacker. He admitted it!"

"How interesting," said Doan.

"Interesting! It's criminal! If I only knew his name I'd report him. I asked him what he was doing to serve his country in this emergency and he said, 'Nothing.' I asked him what he intended to do in the future and he said, 'Less.' Have you ever heard of anything like that?"

"Never in my life," said Doan. "Did you tell him you were going to join the WAACs?"

"Yes."

"What did he say to that?"

"He asked me if they knew it."

"Do they?"

"Well, no. I put in an application, but they haven't replied to it. Naturally they'll accept me."

"Naturally," Doan agreed.

"I told that to this horrible person. I told him that no matter how degrading and disgusting the work they assigned me might be, I would smile and serve."

"What did he say to that?"

"He just said, ''Oh, God,' in a very disgusted tone. I didn't mind the profanity, although I think it's bad taste. It was the sentiment behind it I disapproved of. I told him so, very emphatically. I explained to him the duties and responsibilities we owe our country for the glorious privilege of being one of its citizens."

"Then what?"

"He stopped the car and told me to get out. He said he wanted to vomit, and he always vomited in private if he could manage it. He literally pushed me out! Right on this deserted road in the middle of the desert! And then drove off and left me!"

"You said you didn't know his name," Doan remarked. "Haven't got any idea where he hangs out, have you?"

"No. Are you going to try to find him and teach him to respect patriotic American womanhood?"

"Well, not exactly," Doan said. "I think maybe I could use a slacker like he is in my business"

"What is it—your business?"

"It's rather confidential."

"Oh!" said Harriet Hathaway, thrilled. "It's government work, isn't it?"

"Not unless you're thinking of a different government than I think you are."

"Oh, I know you can't say anything about it," said Harriet understandingly. "I'll just bet you're an agent of some kind or other."

"Of some kind or other," Doan agreed. "Other, to be strictly accurate."

"You can trust my discretion, Mr. Doan. I know just What's that queer noise?" She turned around. "There's a dog in your back seat!"

"I noticed that," Doan told her.

"He's awfully big."

"Yes," said Doan.

"He's snoring"

Doan sighed. "Yes."

"He's a Great Dane"

"So his pedigree says."

"I don't like Great Danes. They're stupid, and they're a nuisance."

"You're telling me."

"Then why did you buy this one?"

"I didn't. I won him in a crap game."

"I don't believe in gambling. You might lose."

"I did," said Doan. "The only trouble was that I didn't know it at the time. I thought I'd won something pretty fancy until I got him home and he started sneering at me and snubbing me because I didn't have a ten-room suite in the penthouse of the Park-Plaza Hotel."

"I know. Then, later, you grew so fond of him and he of you that you couldn't part with him."

"What?" said Doan. "Fond? I detest him, and he despises me."

"Oh, no," said Harriet confidently. "Dogs always love their masters."

"Explain that to Carstairs sometime when you're not busy. It would be an interesting new theory to him."

"Does he always sleep like this?"

"Turn around again," Doan said.

Harriet turned around. Carstairs' broad, blunt muzzle was just a half inch from the end of her nose, and his eyes were fiery greenish slits staring unblinkingly into hers.

"Oh!" she gasped.

"Relax, stupid," said Doan.

The rear seat springs bonged as Carstairs hurled himself back into the cushions again.

"Oh," said Harriet, swallowing. "Oh."

"He gets resentful when people make disparaging remarks about him," Doan explained.

"Oh, I'm sorry! I didn't know he could understand . . . Why, he can't understand! Dogs can't understand what people are saying!"

Doan shrugged. "Okay."

"You signaled him some way. I know! You mentioned his name!"

"Have it your way"

"Well, I don't like him"

"He'd feel insulted if you did. What did this horrible person who picked you up in Masterville look like?"

"Well, he was tall and skinny and unhealthy looking, and he had a beard that grew in patches in a disgustingly unkempt manner. He was really most unpleasant, and I didn't bother to pay much attention to him. I always say we should ignore the lower elements of the population and concentrate our attention on people of culture and breeding."

"I'll bet."

"Bet what?"

"That you always say that."

After that they rode in silence for awhile. Doan turned on the headlights, and the car moved smoothly and silently through the white tunnel they dug in the night. A few stars came out. In the Mojave the stars aren't coy. They don't twinkle and wink at you. They just stare. Sometimes, when you've been alone too long, you begin to think they're taking an altogether too personal interest in you and your affairs, and then you get sand-silly and start running in circles and screaming.

Carstairs licked Doan on the back of the neck. Carstairs' tongue, spread out flat, was as wide as a four-inch paint brush and had much the same effect when used judicially. It never failed to make Doan jump. Now the car swooped across to the wrong side of the road and back again.

"Damn you!" Doan said emphatically.

"What?" Harriet asked, startled.

"Carstairs," Doan explained. "He has an urgent personal errand to attend to."

He stopped the car and shut off the motor, palming the ignition key as he did so. He got out and opened the rear door.

"Come on. And don't step on a rattlesnake, like I hope you will."

Carstairs looked up the road and down the road and snorted twice disapprovingly and then ambled off into the shadows. Doan walked around to the back of the car and stared up at the stars without much enthusiasm. He looked down after a moment, his eyes caught by the gleam of the chrome handle on the trunk compartment.

It was still turned sideways. Doan attempted to turn it back to the locked position. Something was holding it. It was something soft that gave slightly under pressure.

Doan opened the compartment curiously. It had a light in it that snapped on as he did so and showed the man in the compartment quite plainly. He was sitting down, his knees doubled up, and his head twisted back sideways. It was the middle finger of his left hand that had kept the compartment from locking. The edge of the lock had roweled the skin and flesh across the knuckle, but it wasn't bleeding.

Doan let his breath out slowly and quietly, and then breathed in as slowly. The man had been stabbed expertly in the side of his throat, and blood was caked thick and scaly all over the front of his coat. He was not a large man and not young. His suit, where the blood hadn't stained it, was blue, and it looked as though it hadn't fitted well even when he was alive.

Carstairs came out of the shadows. He paused for a second and then peered around Doan and sniffed once. He backed off two steps, his upper lip curling.

"I know," said Doan. "He's not fresh. I wonder just what kind of a story I'm going to tell Arne that will account for me picking up a three-day dead hitchhiker with a sliced jugular vein."

Carstairs watched him silently.

"The compartment was unlocked," Doan said absently, "and he could have been shoved in there any place I stopped, only I didn't stop any place where there weren't a lot of people around . . ." He paused and looked toward the front of the car. "Maybe I'm getting softening of the brain."

He closed the compartment, after gingerly shoving the lax, leaden-tinged hand out of the way, and made sure it was locked this time.

"Get in," he said.

Carstairs climbed quickly and silently into the backseat. Doan closed the door after him and got in the front seat and started the car.

"This horrible person," he said, rolling the car back on the highway, "the one who picked you up, where did he go after he put you down?"

"On along the road," Harriet said. "The same way we've been going."

"He didn't stop or come back, did he?"

"No."

"You didn't see anyone else sort of prowling around in the vicinity while you were waiting, did you?"

"No," she said blankly. "Why?"

"Just wondered," Doan answered. "Did you have any friends with you, back there when I picked you up, someone who might have been temporarily mislaid in the brush or something?"

"Friends?"

"Chums. Acquaintances. Traveling companions."

"Of course not."

"Oh," said Doan. He waited for awhile. "We're coming into Heliotrope in a couple of hours. That's as far as I'm going. Would you take it amiss if I put on my best manners and invited you to have dinner with me?"

Harriet considered. "I think it would be perfectly proper for me to have dinner with you, Mr. Doan."

"I'm glad," said Doan.

Chapter 4

HELIOTROPE IS TOO FAR INLAND TO FALL UNDER the restrictions of the coastal dim-out zone, and since the taste of the advertising portion of its population runs toward the more violent shades of neon, it resembles a string of cheap jewelry tucked in against the dark and barren sweep of the Crazy Leg Mountains when approached at night from the floor of the desert. Its main street is four blocks long, paved at the sides but not in the middle, and at close range the signs on the buildings that line it are so blinding that it is hard for the stranger to tell whether he has arrived in a town or at the Fourth of July.

Doan parked the Cadillac in the unpaved section of the street midway between the Double-Eagle Hotel (golden neon eagle flapping its wings in two-four time) and the Bar B Grill (fiendish twenty-foot red flames lapping around a bored blue cow). The combination of colors gave Harriet Hathaway's healthy face a tinge that reminded him urgently of the cargo he was carrying in the trunk compartment.

"Let's try that," he said, indicating the Bar B. "They might really have steaks."

"I'd like one," said Harriet.

Doan opened the door for Carstairs, and the three of them crossed the street and went in through the red bordered swing doors. The place was long and low and L-shaped, filled to capacity with a bar and round, blacktopped tables. The only person in sight was the bartender. He had gold front teeth and only one ear.

"Have you any steaks tonight?" Doan asked.

"Sure," said the bartender.

"Are they good?"

"I dunno, mister. I just cook 'em. I don't eat 'em."

Doan selected a table, and pulled out a chair for Harriet Hathaway. "We'll take a chance. Give us a couple of what you think are New York cuts and some French fried potatoes and a salad bowl."

"Ain't you gonna have anything to drink first?" the bartender asked. "We don't make any profit on our food, you know. We can't run this dive unless we sell liquor."

Doan looked inquiringly at Harriet. "You?"

"I don't drink, thank you."

Doan nodded at the bartender. "I'll have a triple bourbon in a beer glass."

"Why?" said the bartender.

Carstairs had collapsed beside the table, and Doan indicated him meaningly.

"I'm only allowed one drink before meals, unless I want an argument."

The bartender stared. "You mean you let a dog dictate to you?"

"Up-si-daisy," said Doan.

Carstairs got up instantly. Doan pointed toward the bar, and Carstairs swung his head slowly in the direction.

"Hey!" said the bartender. "Hold it, now! I didn't mean any offense. I was just making a remark, and I can see that there's a lot to be said for your point of view."

"Let's have a little less conversation and a little more service," Doan requested.

"Sure. Tell him to lie down again like a nice dog, would you mind?"

"Boom," said Doan.

Carstairs relaxed his muscles and hit the floor all at once.

"One triple bourbon in a beer glass," the bartender said, becoming briskly businesslike. "Yes, sir. Coming right up. Two New York cuts, side of fried and grass. On the fire."

He brought the drink for Doan, making a careful detour around Carstairs, and then went back and began to bustle busily around the hooded grill at the far end of the bar. Doan raised the glass to take a sip of the whiskey in it and then paused, staring at the man who had materialized from somewhere or other and was now standing beside the table smiling at him.

"How do you do?" said the man.

He was small, and he had a round, olive-skinned face with a dimple in each cheek, and his teeth were very white and even under a pencil-line black mustache. His eyes were liquidly dark and sparkling. He wore a brown suit and a brown shirt and tie and had a brown handkerchief peeping artistically out of the breast pocket of his coat.

"All right," said Doan.

The small man turned his head and looked at Harriet. There was nothing insulting about his look. It was courteously calculating, nothing more.

"Would you like to buy a blonde?" he asked, turning back to Doan.

"A what?" Doan said.

"A blonde."

"No," said Doan.

"A brunette?"

"No," said Doan. "Supposing you go away and sit down somewhere."

The small man smiled winningly. "You don't approve of me, perhaps?"

"Not perhaps. Positively."

"You scorn me?"

"That's right."

The small man bowed precisely. "Good evening." He turned on his heel and walked back to the farthest table in the rear corner of the room and sat down.

Harriet said, "He's such a handsome little man, but he must be

awfully drunk. I mean, who ever heard of buying a blonde or brunette
. . . Oh!"

"Yes," said Doan.

"You mean he—they—you . . . Oh!"

"Oh," Doan agreed.

"Why, that's terrible! Why, I'm going to call a policeman and have
him arrested!"

"It wouldn't do any good. They'd just have to bail him out or pay
his fine."

"They! You mean, they pay . . . Oh, that's horrible! Oh, I don't
believe . . . Really?"

"Yes."

"Well, I'm going to..." Her voice trailed away. She was staring
glassy-eyed over Doan's shoulder. "Oh, there he is! You!"

Doan turned around. A tall man in khaki pants and shirt and leather
jacket was halfway between the door and the bar. He had stopped so
suddenly that he had one foot still half-raised to take another step. He
was wearing black—not dark, but black—glasses, and he had an unkempt, patchy beard about an inch long at its best points. He was watching Harriet Hathaway with the sort of expression the ordinary person
reserves for a nest of rattlesnakes.

"That's the horrible slacker person," Harriet explained to Doan.
"You! Come right over here!"

The tall man put the raised foot carefully in back of the one he was
standing on. Harriet got out of her chair.

"Don't you dare try to avoid me! You come here! I want to speak
to you!"

That last did it. The tall man spun like a top and dove for the door.
He hit it and was gone with a double whack-whack to mark his pas-
sage.

"Oh, he's not going to get away from me again!" said Harriet, and
went right after him.

The doors whack-whacked again, even more emphatically. Carstairs
had raised his head and was looking at Doan with an expression of
long-suffering annoyance. Doan shrugged and took a big drink of bourbon.

"So you wanna insult my friend, do you?"

Doan looked up slowly. This man was wearing a ten-gallon hat

and a blue bandanna and a calfskin vest and brass-studded chaps, and
the effect was so startling it was grotesque. His face didn't match the
camouflage. It was a fat, florid face with black, beady chips for eyes. It
was blurred just slightly. It looked like a face someone had drawn and
then half erased. In other words, it looked like a fifth rate prizefighter's
face.

"So you wanna insult my friend, huh?" he said again.

"Sure," said Doan, putting his glass down.

The man was as thick as he was wide, and he turned and pointed
meaningly toward the back of the room. "That's my friend, what you
insulted."

"Go away while you're healthy," said Doan. "Take him with you."

The thick man clipped him with a short right. It was an expertly
professional blow, coming without any warning at all. Doan had just
time to tilt his head a quarter inch, so that the splayed, thick knuckles
landed on his cheekbone instead of on the point of his jaw.

The force of the blow knocked him clear out of his chair and flat on
the floor. He rolled over and dove, not for the thick man, but for Carstairs.
He was just in time. He got a stranglehold on Carstairs' neck with one
arm and jerked his front feet out from under him with the other.

Carstairs sprawled down, half on top of him, making little grunting
thick sounds deep in his throat.

"Stop it!" Doan panted, rapping him sharply on the top of the head.
"Did I ask for help? Did I? Relax!"

The thick man laughed jeeringly. "Look at this! I hit the guy, so he
hits his dog! A screwball!"

Doan got up. "That was a cute trick," he said amiably. "What would
you do if I did this?"

He made a fork out of the first two fingers of his right hand and
then flicked the fingers at the thick man's eyes. Just exactly like Laurel
and Hardy. Only Doan meant it. One of his fingers bit the thick man in
each of his eyes.

The thick man screamed and slapped both palms against his eyes.
Doan stepped back two paces and then forward one and kicked the
thick man six inches below his belt. The thick man stopped screaming
right in mid-note and doubled up. Doan hit him in the back of his neck
with a full-arm swing, and the thick man followed his nose right down
to the floor and squirmed there on his stomach.

Doan stepped back three paces this time and then forward two and jumped. He came down heels first, lumberjack style, on the thick man's back. There was a dull little crack, and then the thick man didn't squirm any more. He didn't do anything. He lay where he was.

Doan stepped off him lightly and looked at the back of the room. "And now I want a word with you."

The small man had lost his neat and glistening smile and the best part of his olive complexion. He looked decidedly ill. He was standing up, flat against the wall, and now he shook a thin clasp knife out of the sleeve of his neat brown suit and opened the blade with a flick of his wrist.

Doan picked up the chair he had fallen out of and walked slowly toward him. The small man threw the knife in a sudden wickering blur. Doan caught it on the bottom of the chair, and it stuck there with a steely thrum. He worked it loose and balanced it in his right hand thoughtfully.

The small man didn't wait for any decisions. He dove head first through the window behind his table. Doan stared at the window as though he had never seen one before. He took three steps toward it, craning his neck, and then suddenly whipped around and dropped into a crouch, facing the other way.

The bartender was standing at attention, both hands raised over his head. "Oh, no!" he said quickly. "No, sir! I'm neutral, thanks."

Doan watched him.

"Mister," said the bartender, "this position ain't very comfortable, but I ain't gonna twitch an eyelid until you say I can."

"All right," said Doan. "Who was the gent who went out the window?"

"Name of Free-Look Jones. No friend of mine."

"Where does he live?"

"I dunno."

"Find out," said Doan, "before I count three. One, two—"

"On Rosewater Lane," said the bartender quickly. "It runs out north of town. He lives in a shack next to a wrecked dump truck near the end. There's no number."

"Okay," said Doan. "Sweep up the garbage on the floor. I'll be back."

"Don't hurry," said the bartender.

Chapter 5

ROSEWATER LANE STARTED OUT WITH QUITE a splurge. It was paved, and there were four houses in the first block. The second block was only half paved and contained three houses. The third block didn't have any pavement or any houses, either, and after that the lane circled in a discouraged way around a knoll, and there was the abandoned dump truck like some armored prehistoric bug that had been tipped over on its back and decided to make the best of it.

The shack was low and unpainted and swaybacked, pushed in against the darker blot of the knoll. There were no lights showing, and Doan stopped the Cadillac a hundred yards away from it and opened the rear door.

"Take a look," he ordered. He pointed at the shack and made a circling motion with his forefinger.

Carstairs got out of the car and faded quietly and expertly into the darkness. Doan waited. After about five minutes Carstairs came back and put his front feet on the running board and snuffled over the lowered glass.

"Okay," said Doan.

He got out of the car and went around to the back and opened the trunk compartment. The man inside hadn't changed any, for the better or the worse. Doan took hold of his arm and pulled. The man slid out of the compartment with a horribly fluid laxness and sprawled all over the ground.

Doan said some things to himself in an undertone. He leaned down and picked the man up, trying to avoid the dried blood, and then carried him toward the shack with Carstairs coursing on ahead alertly. The front, and only, door had a padlock and hasp on it, but the padlock had rusted open. Doan maneuvered it off the hasp with the toe of one shoe and then kicked the door open.

He turned sideways and slid through the door, still carrying the dead man. Inside the darkness was as thick and smooth as molasses, but it had considerably more odor. Carstairs snorted disapprovingly. Letting his burden slide down to the floor, Doan struck a match.

The flame reflected in a little sparkle from the unshaded electric light bulb that hung from the ceiling on a limp yellow cord. Doan pulled the string attached to it, and the darkness retired, quivering malignantly, to the corners of the room.

There was a table with a stained and splintered top just under the light, and there were two tin cups and two tin plates and two forks, all dirty, on top of it. Doan regarded the setup thoughtfully for a moment, and then picked up the dead man, and put him in the swaybacked chair in front of one of the plates and maneuvered his arms and legs around carefully until he stayed there.

Doan stepped back to look things over, his head tilted in a specula-tive way. He was frowning a little. Then his eye caught a battered deck of cards resting between two old gin bottles on a board that had been nailed against the far wall to form a shelf. He picked the cards up and ran through them quickly. They were marked with invisible little nicks along the edges.

Doan smiled. He piled the tin plates and cups at one end of the table and then scattered the cards over its surface, letting a few fall on the floor.

He stepped back and surveyed the scene again. Things looked a little better. He took Free-Look Jones' knife from his pocket and wiped the blade and handle carefully on his handkerchief and then, still using his handkerchief to cover his hand, he put the point of the knife against the purple-edged wound in the dead man's neck and pushed.

The blade went in slickly and easily up to its hilt. Doan let go. The handle of the knife was made of some green composition material that caught the light and glittered sinisterly, sticking out under the lax line of the dead man's jaw.

Doan nodded to himself, satisfied. He pulled the string on the light bulb and felt his way toward the door. He bumped into Carstairs in front of it and said, "Go on. Outside."

He shut the front door and put the rusted padlock back on its hasp, and then headed for the car with Carstairs trailing along behind in dis-approving silence. Doan began to whistle to himself in a mildly pleased way.

He pushed Carstairs into the back seat, turned the car around, and headed back for the center of town. Things were looking up a bit now. The signs were brighter, if possible, and parts of the populace, prowling like zombies in the weird light, sauntered aimlessly and stared or merely stood, hip-shot and dejected on the corners, smoking hand-rolled cigarettes and spitting in the gutters. Cars, with sand on their hoods and spades lashed over the front fenders, were parked in thick clusters in the street center.

Doan found a place for the Cadillac, and he and Carstairs got out and walked across to the Bar B Grill. The one-eared bartender was still in sole charge, and he sighed deeply and began to clatter bottles around in a very absorbed manner when Doan and Carstairs appeared.

"Mr. Doan!" Harriet Hathaway called. "You've come back again!"

"I think you're right," Doan said.

She was sitting at the table she and Doan had occupied before, and the man with the black glasses was sitting opposite her. He was eating a steak, but he didn't look as though he were enjoying it. His shoulders were hunched, and he had the numbly suffering air of a man unbearably buffeted by fate.

"This is Mr. Blue, Mr. Doan," Harriet said. "He's eating your steak."

"That's thoughtful of him," Doan remarked.

"I didn't want to eat it," Blue said.

"Nonsense," said Harriet. "Of course you did."

"I don't like steak."

Harriet laughed. "Now isn't that a silly thing to say! Everyone likes steak. And besides, it's good for you. You just go right ahead and enjoy it."

"All right," said Blue glumly. He put another piece in his mouth and chewed with grim concentration.

"You seem to be getting along a little better than you were at last reports," Doan observed.

Harriet laughed again. "It was all a mistake. It was just because Mr. Blue is so ignorant."

Blue looked up at Doan and nodded solemnly, his blacked-out glasses winking in the light. "I sure am. I'm awful ignorant, Mr. Doan."

"Is that so?" said Doan.

Harriet said, "He didn't even know there was a war! He really didn't. He can't read, and he doesn't have money enough to buy a radio, and he's so shy he never talks to people. Isn't that incredible?"

"Yes," said Doan.

"You know," Harriet said, "he thought when I was talking to him before about the emergency that I meant the depression! And when I told him about the WAACs, he thought I was referring to the WPA!"

"Did he?" said Doan.

"But when I explained things, he became very interested at once. Didn't you become interested?"

"Yes, ma'am," said Blue, starting stubbornly on another piece of steak.

"When I told him about our brave boys fighting in all parts of the world on land and on the sea and in the air, he was astounded. Weren't you?"

"Uh-huh," said Blue. "Sure was."

"Won't you sit down, Mr. Doan?" Harriet asked. "I'm just going to describe to Mr. Blue the wonderful work our Air Force has been doing. I'm fascinated by the Air Force, and I know all about it. Wouldn't you like to listen, too?"

"Thank you, no," said Doan. "I have a little business to look after. Perhaps I'll see you later."

He went over to the bar and drummed on it with his fingers.

"Want some whiskey?" the bartender asked, staying at a safe distance.

"No. You. Come here."

"You ain't mad, are you?"

"No."

The bartender slid a little closer, keeping an eye on Carstairs. "What?"

"Where'd you dump the debris I left here?"

"Oh, him. I called Doc Gravelmeyer to look at him, and the doc took him over to his office. I wouldn't want to offer any advice or anything, but if I was you I'd sort of step over and look into that situation."

"Why?"

"Well, Doc Gravelmeyer has been readin' a book again, and when he was over here he was talkin' about acute something-or-other that I didn't like the sound of. He said right away that Parsley Jack—that's the guy you tangled with—looked like a first-class incipient case of it and that he'd better open Jack up and look around a bit. Now the trouble with Doc Gravelmeyer is that he's liable to get so interested when he gets to prowlin' around that it's sometimes fatal."

"I should worry."

"You're right," said the bartender, "you should. Doc's the coroner. The last guy that kicked off while he was operatin' on him got listed as an accidental death due to drowning in a sand storm. Doc is a very humorous guy sometimes."

"He sounds like it. Where can I find him?"

"His office is down the street over the undertaker's parlor. Does the undertaker, too. Just for a laugh, he claims he always gets you, comin' or goin'."

"Ha-ha," said Doan sourly. "Come on, Carstairs." They went out into the street again, but Doan didn't attempt to find Doc Gravelmeyer's office. Instead, he went to the Cadillac, got his two suitcases out of the rear seat, and headed for the Double-Eagle Hotel.

He went up the three slick marble steps at the entrance and through the brass bound doors and right back into the nineteenth century. The lobby was two stories high and featured a crystal chandelier as big as a dive bomber, and potentially as dangerous to any innocent bystanders if it happened to fall. There were rubber plants in all the available corners and chairs with red plush upholstery and gilt-knobbed legs, and shiny brass spittoons with gracefully curved necks. All this was overlaid neatly with an odor of fly-spray that made Carstairs sneeze indignantly.

The only concession to the present was the desk clerk. He was as slick and shiny as a new cocktail shaker, and he owned a smile that hit you in the face like a wet towel.

"Yes, sir!" he said.

"I want a room for myself and my friend. Twin beds."

"Yes, sir!" said the clerk. He twirled a big leather-bound register around on the desk and pointed a pen at Doan.

Doan signed as "I. Doanwashi, Tokyo, Japan."

The clerk didn't bat an eye. "Glad to have you with us, Mr. Doanwashi. I hope you enjoy your stay. Joshua! Joshua! Front!"

A man came out of the door at the rear of the lobby. He was a very small, very frail man, wearing a uniform that would have enabled him to join a Civil War infantry regiment without attracting undue attention. He leaned over the desk and held out his hand blindly. The clerk slapped a key into his palm.

"Two-one-four."

"Two-one-four," Joshua repeated numbly.

He leaned over to pick up Doan's bags and fell flat on his face. He got up carefully, took a deep breath, and picked up the bags. He headed for the red carpeted stairway in a wavering, loose-kneed quickstep. He missed by ten feet and disappeared in the shadows under the staircase.

The clerk smiled amiably at Doan. There was a crash and a thud, and Joshua backed out into the lobby and made another run at the stairs. He hit them this time, and got halfway up before he lost his momentum. He turned around and sat down with a baffled sigh.

"Two-one-four," said the clerk.

"Two-one-four," Joshua echoed obediently.

He got up and picked up the bags again, and made it to the top of the staircase. Doan and Carstairs followed him with due caution. Joshua had dropped the bags halfway down the straight, high-ceilinged hall, and was bent over in front of a door, jabbing at the middle panel with the key the clerk had given him.

"Here," said Doan.

He took the key and unlocked the door. Joshua dove head first into the darkened room. Doan waited. Nothing happened. Finally Doan groped around the edge of the door until he found the light switch and turned it.

Joshua was sitting on the edge of one of the high brass beds. He had his elbows on his knees and his chin resting in his hands. Doan picked up the suitcases and brought them inside the room.

"Thanks, bud," said Joshua. "Open the windows before you go, and leave a call for me at ten-thirty."

"Okay," said Doan.

He took hold of Joshua by the slack of his uniform jacket and marched him to the door and pushed. Joshua fell in a graceful heap in the middle of the hall. Doan shut the door and looked at Carstairs.

"Well, you can't blame me for that, surely," he said.

Carstairs was sitting in the middle of the floor. He watched Doan levelly for a moment and then closed his eyes and sighed with long-suffering patience.

Doan took the .25 automatic out of his pocket and shoved it under the mattress of one of the beds. He straightened his tie in front of the wavery mirror over the dresser, and then nodded at Carstairs.

"Come to, soup-brain. I think we better move around a bit."

He opened the door and looked out. Joshua had disappeared. Doan and Carstairs went down the hall and downstairs to the lobby.

The clerk still smiled. "I hope you found your room satisfactory?"

"Very," said Doan. "Where's Joshua?"

"He went out for a few minutes to get a drink of root beer."

"Root beer?" Doan said. "Joshua?"

"Yes. He makes it himself in the back of a drugstore next door."

"I'll bet," said Doan. "I want to use your telephone to make a long distance call."

"If you'll give me the number, I'll get it for you. You can take it in the booth over there."

"I'd rather use your board. Haven't you got an errand you can run?"

"No," said the clerk. "But I can use these." He took a pair of rubber earplugs from his pocket and inserted them in his ears.

"There's a scorpion on your shirt collar," Doan told him.

The clerk removed one of the plugs. "What?"

"Those are fine," Doan said. He sat down in front of the board and flipped the switch that connected with the exchange, holding the half-headset receiver to his ear.

"Hello Gerald, darling," a feminine voice greeted.

"Gerald's busy not listening to you at the moment," Doan said. "Is there any message?"

"No! What are you doing on the board?"

"Trying to put in a long distance call to Brighton 7-7345. That's an exchange in Brighton outside of New York City. Will you get it for me?"

"I suppose so."

"And don't bother to listen in after you get it. I'm a Japanese spy, and the things I'm going to say are confidential military information."

"Nothing you could say would interest me in the slightest, I assure you. Hold the line."

Doan listened through a long series of clicks and buzzes and dribbles of conversation. Finally the operator said, "Here's your party, and you're welcome to him."

"Hello, hello," said a masculine voice. "Hello. This is A. Truegold, president of Severn International Detectives."

"You won't be for long," Doan said, "if you make any more lend-lease deals with me for the subject or object or whatever."

"Oh. So it's you. Now Doan, nobody asked me to loan you to them. They told me. You want I should argue with the Army and Navy?"

"All right. Send five hundred dollars to I. Doanwashi, care of the Double-Eagle Hotel in Heliotrope, Nevada or California. Telegraph it right away."

"Now Doan, you're already drawn ahead three months. You can't expect to draw any more when you aren't even working for me. Why don't you be reasonable?"

"Why don't you stop arguing? You know you'll lose. Send the dough tonight. I'm trying to raffle off a used cadaver, and I need it for operating capital."

"Doan! A what did you say?"

"Skip it. Just forget the whole matter. Only don't start yelling for me when the cops come rapping on your door and asking about stray bodies."

"Doan! You didn't involve the agency in a murder? That's against our policy! It says so right on our stationery!"

"Show it to the police."

"Doan! Wait a minute! Don't you dare hang up on me! What name did you say you were using?"

"I. Doanwashi."

"Why?"

"I'm a Japanese spy now."

"Don't say things like that! Do you want to get us both shot? Doan! Are you drunk?"

"Stinking. I'm liable to start babbling and drooling at any moment."

"Oh, Doan! Now please. You've got no right to involve me or the agency . . . All right! I'll send it. But no more! I warn you! I won't tolerate any further blackmail from you!"

"Okay. Is that little greasy bird who used to collect filthy postcards still hanging out in Des Moines?"

"Meredith? Yes. Why?"

"I want you to call him tonight, as soon as you send me my dough, and tell him to send a telegram to Harriet Hathaway in care of the Double-Eagle Hotel in Heliotrope, Nevada or California, whichever he knows how to spell. Have him tell her in the telegram to stay here until she is contacted for important detached confidential duty. Have him sign it with just his initials and last name, and tell him to put the letters

C-A-P-T in front of the name. That stands for capitals."

"It stands for something else, too," said Truegold. "It stands for captain."

"Does it?" Doan asked.

"Doan! I won't do it! No!"

Doan cut the connection and nodded at the clerk.

The clerk removed his earplugs. "Did you get your party?"

"Yes. Put the charge on my room bill. Do you know anyone named Dust-Mouth Haggerty?"

"Not socially," said the clerk.

"I wasn't looking for a formal introduction. Where would I be likely to find him?"

"In jail."

"You mean right now?"

"Almost any time."

"Thanks," said Doan. "I'll go take a look." He snapped his fingers at Carstairs and started for the front door.

A woman, trailed by a faint, dim shadow, came in and stopped short, staring at him. Doan stared back. He couldn't have helped himself had he tried. She was beautifully tall and beautifully slender, and she had shoulder length black hair that gleamed darker and deeper and smoother than polished ebony. She had features so unbelievably perfect they made you gulp and look again, and then keep right on gulping. She was wearing white linen slacks, and a white jacket trimmed with big brass buttons, and white open-toed pumps, and a red sash around her waist. She pulled all the life out of the lobby and focused it on herself, like a little boy sucking soda through a straw.

"No," she said, and her voice was soft and just slightly hoarse. "There couldn't be two pair like you."

"If I wasn't looking right at it," Doan answered, "I wouldn't believe there could even be one like you"

The faint, dim shadow behind the woman tiptoed closer and peered over her shoulder. The shadow owned a pair of wide, worried eyes and a long nose, and sported a white catalogue sombrero with a high crown circled by a purple and red band four inches wide.

"A fat little number," said the woman, "with a big mouth and a bigger dog. Wasn't that it?"

"Now, Sally," said the shadow. "Now, wait. There must be some reasonable explanation."

Susan Sally glided forward three smooth steps. "I don't like fat little numbers. Especially fat little numbers that call me fat." She paused meaningly. "I don't like big dogs, either."

Carstairs promptly walked around behind Doan.

"You coward," Doan muttered. He smiled nervously. "I'm sorry about that. It was a mistake."

"That's okay," Susan Sally said amiably. "Let's shake on it, huh?"

She held out her right hand. Doan reached for it, but didn't take it. Instead he shoved her right elbow back and up with the heel of his palm. She had started to move just as soon as he had. She swung a full roundhouse left at his face. The shove pushed her off balance, and her fist swished harmlessly past in front of Doan's nose. She staggered a little, and Doan caught both her wrists, holding her upright, facing him. He was watching her feet.

The shadow was gibbering and screeching in the background. "Hit her in the stomach!"

"What?" said Doan, startled.

The shadow jiggled both fists in an agony of apprehension. "Not in the face! Don't hit her face! Thirty-five hundred dollars a week!"

Susan Sally was standing perfectly still, perfectly relaxed. Doan didn't let go of her wrists.

"That doesn't fool me, either," he said. "And if you try a faint, I'll just step out of the way and let you flop,"

"You think of everything, honey," said Susan Sally. "Let's have a peace conference, huh?"

"Sure," said Doan, still holding her wrists.

"I mean it."

Doan let go. "Okay. I'm really sorry I said you were fat. I apologize."

She winked at him. "I knew you didn't mean it. After all, you've got eyes, haven't you? I was just griped because you walked off with my special steak. What did you want it ground up for?"

Doan pointed at Carstairs. "For him."

"You mean, he ate it all?"

"Sure."

"Come on out, large and loop-legged," she said, "and let me look at you."

Carstairs sidled cautiously out from behind Doan.

"You're not bad," Susan Sally said. "Only you're not worth a three-pound steak. Walk off with another one of mine, and I'll kick your teeth in."

Carstairs looked impressed."

"'MacAdoo!" said Susan Sally.

The shadow with the big hat answered eagerly, "Yes, Sally?"

"Trot out the etiquette."

MacAdoo cleared his throat. "This is Miss Susan Sally, internationally famous star of the stage and screen. And may I ask your name, sir?"

"Just call me Doan for short."

"Miss Sally, may I present Mr. Doan—a humble admirer of your art."

"Hi, toots," said Susan Sally.

"Hi," said Doan. "Who's the echo on my left?"

"Just a stooge," said Susan Sally. "I tote him around for laughs."

"I am Miss Sally's business manager and agent," said MacAdoo. "Elmer A. MacAdoo is the name. I'm very happy to make your acquaintance."

"Pipe down," Susan Sally told him. "What's your line, Doan? Aside from stealing steaks."

"I'm a Japanese spy."

"How's business?"

"All shot to hell. We tried to float a loan, but it sank."

"Maybe you can pump out the Pacific and recover your investment. Let's go have a slug of *sake,* Doan."

"It's an idea," Doan admitted. "We'll toast the Emperor."

"Over a slow fire," Susan Sally agreed.

A new voice said, "Excuse me, please."

The man had come up so quietly they hadn't noticed him. He was the type of person it was easy not to notice. He was small and dusty and shriveled, and he had a long drooping black mustache and round, solemn blue eyes. He had a nickel-plated star pinned to his coat collar.

"Excuse you for what?" Doan asked.

"Excuse me for botherin' you. But I think I'm gonna have to arrest you. Do you mind?"

"Not at all," said Doan.

The man tapped himself on his thin chest. "Peterkin is the name. Ask anybody. I'm the sheriff. Ask Miss Sally."

"Hello, scum," said Susan Sally.

"Right nice to see you again, Miss Sally," Peterkin said humbly. "You went and parked your car in a red zone, and I have to give you a ticket."

Susan Sally snapped her fingers in MacAdoo's direction. He produced a shiny new dime and handed it to Peterkin.

"Thank you, Miss Sally," Peterkin said. "I'll sure tear that ticket right up."

"You sure better had. And remember it gives only a nickel for the next one."

"Yes, ma'am."

Harriet Hathaway ran in through the front door. "Mr. Doan! Oh, I've been looking everywhere! You didn't pay the bill at the restaurant, and Mr. Blue doesn't have any money, and the man won't let Mr. Blue go until the bill is paid, and I'm not through telling him about the Air Force yet, either!"

"It's a problem," Doan agreed. He squinted thoughtfully for a moment and then took out his wallet and gave Harriet a five-dollar bill. "Here. And would you mind taking care of Carstairs for a little while?"

"That nasty, ugly thing!" Harriet said. "Yes, I would!"

Carstairs leered at her malignantly.

Susan Sally slapped him across the muzzle. "Mind your manners!"

Carstairs backed up, staring at Susan Sally with an expression of ludicrously incredulous amazement.

"Yeah," she said. "I mean you."

Carstairs sat down and blinked at her, obviously trying to think of some solution to the situation. He couldn't. He decided to ignore it. He lay down on the floor with great dignity and commenced to snore ostentatiously.

"But I don't want to take care of him!" Harriet wailed. "I hate him!"

"I'll help you," Susan Sally told her. "Doan, who's this fugitive from a select seminary?"

"Harriet Hathaway," Doan said.

MacAdoo stepped forward and cleared his throat. "This is Miss Susan Sally, internationally famous star of the stage and screen. Miss

Sally, may I present Miss Hathaway, a humble—"

"How do you do," Harriet said absently. "Mr. Doan, how long are you going to be gone?"

Doan looked at Peterkin. "What am I arrested for?"

"Attempted murder, I guess."

"A couple of hours," Doan said to Harriet.

"Well, I suppose I can—Wh-what? Arrested?"

"Just a formality," Doan soothed.

"A-attempted murder?"

" Not a very good attempt," said Doan.

"But—but—but—Oh, Mr. Doan!"

"Take a deep breath, kiddie," Susan Sally said, "and mama will let you tell her all about the cute little Air Force. See you in jail, Doan."

Chapter 6

DOAN AND PETERKIN CAME OUT OF THE Double Eagle Hotel and walked north along the main street toward the older and dimmer part of town.

"You want I should walk behind you?" Peterkin asked. "So people won't know you're arrested-like?"

"I can stand it if you can," Doan told him. "I was thinking of going to jail anyway as soon as I got around to it. Is Dust-Mouth Haggerty there?"

"I don't know."

"Who could I ask that would?"

"Oh, we'll find out when we get there. Dust-Mouth checks in and out at sort of odd hours."

"I see," said Doan. "Why?"

"He lives there."

"Lives in jail?" Doan asked.

"Yup," said Peterkin.

"All right," said Doan. "Why?"

"Well, he ain't got no place else to live."

"Sure," said Doan. "Why?"

"The government went and stole his claim. That was an awful dirty trick to play on Dust-Mouth. He never did any harm to anybody. He never even voted in his life."

Doan sighed. "Okay. Do you know a character by the name of Free-Look Jones?"

"Sure."

"What business is he in?"

"He's a private detective."

Doan stopped short. "Oh, now wait a minute."

"I guess he has a couple of other jobs, too," Peterkin admitted. "I guess he's a sort of an agent or salesman in his spare time."

Doan started on again. "I should hope so. You know, I'd keep an eye on him if I were you"

"Would you?" Peterkin inquired, interested.

"Yes. He looks to me like the sort of a guy who would cheat at cards."

"Oh, he does. All the time."

"What if someone caught him at it?"

"He'd run, likely."

"Maybe he might not," Doan said. "Maybe he'd haul out that knife he carries and use it."

"Maybe," Peterkin agreed gravely.

"A really alert law officer," Doan said, "would sort of think of those things and go out and look over his shack once in awhile."

"What for?" Peterkin asked.

"To see if he could find any—ah—clues."

"What are them?"

"Clues? Evidence."

"Like in court?"

"Sort of."

"Oh," said Peterkin.

They turned into a narrower street that wasn't quite so fearfully lighted. A small, towheaded boy marched toward them. He had his head down and his shoulders hunched, and he was kicking the walk hard with his heels.

"What's the trouble, Joey?" Peterkin asked.

The boy looked at them with his lower lip thrust out an inch. "Aw, them big kids. They won't let me play with 'em. I don't never have no fun."

"Aw, now," Peterkin soothed. "I'll tell you something you can do that'll just be more fun than the dickens."

"What?" said the, boy, skeptically.

"Well, you see that rock over there? Suppose you take that and sneak up on Schmaltz's Variety Store and heave it through the front window. There'll be a big smash and crash, and people will holler and everything."

"Gee," said the boy, entranced.

Doan and Peterkin walked on. The boy was contemplating the rock with glistening, eager eyes.

"You don't like Schmaltz?" Doan asked.

"Huh? Why, sure I do. Schmaltz is one of my friends."

"Why the business with the rock and the window?"

"Oh, that's for the S. E. C."

"Securities Exchange Commission?"

"Nope. Society to Encourage Crime. It's an organization just for police officers."

"Umm," said Doan. "What does it do?"

"Like it says, encourages crime."

"Why?" said Doan wearily.

"Say, did you ever think what would happen if everybody turned honest all of a sudden?"

"No," said Doan.

"All police officers would lose their jobs, that's what! That's why we got the S. E. C. We got to keep a supply of criminals comin' along all the time so there'll be a big demand for police officers. Now you take Joey there. We start 'em out easy, like I did him. He starts bustin' windows. He sees how easy it is. So pretty soon he starts bustin' windows and stealin' the stuff inside. Get it?"

"Oh, sure. Big oaks from little acorns. Does Susan Sally come here very often?"

"Sure. Lots."

"Why?"

"She used to live here. She comes back to sort of show us how wrong we was."

"About what?"

"Well, she used to go around tellin' everybody how pretty she was gonna be when she grew up, and everybody laughed at her because she sure was an ugly little mutt. She ain't now, though."

"I noticed," said Doan. "Who complained on me, anyway? I mean, who asked you to arrest me?"

"Nobody. I thought it up myself. On account of Doc Gravelmeyer told me he was gonna perform a delicate operation on Parsley Jack, and when Doc Gravelmeyer gets to operatin', delicate or otherwise, you just can never tell."

"Did it ever occur to anyone to hop him for malpractice?"

"Doc Gravelmeyer? Oh, you couldn't do that. He used to be an abortionist."

"I'm a little slow this evening," Doan said. "Why would that stop me?"

"You couldn't get him convicted. Half the doctors in the state would testify for him. They'd have to. They used to send him patients, and he can prove it. Doc is a very smart fella in his way."

"This is a nice little town you have here," Doan observed.

"Ain't it, though? Here's the jail. I'll bet you'll like that, too."

It was a square, substantial-looking building with white stucco walls and a red tile roof, and the shiny iron bars on the windows blended in pretty well with the Spanish motif. Someone had spent a lot of time and money landscaping the lawn around it and installing floodlights at strategic intervals.

"Nifty," Doan commented. "For a town this size."

"Yup," said Peterkin proudly. "You see, we might belong to either Nevada or California, so we have to collect taxes for both states. But on the other hand, we might not belong to either one, so of course it would be wrong to pay them the taxes we collect. So we spend 'em on improvements."

"Who's we?"

"Well, me."

"I thought so," said Doan. "Don't you have any competition for this job of yours?"

"Well, there was a couple of guys, but they got sick. Doc Gravelmeyer did his best to save 'em."

"He didn't succeed, though."

"Nope," said Peterkin. He pushed open the heavy black varnished door. "Step right in."

It was a reception room and a very nice one. There was a deep red carpet on the floor and oil paintings on the cream colored walls and a big, flat executive's desk in the far corner. The bald little man behind the desk took off a pair of pince-nez glasses and tapped them against one forefinger in a businesslike way.

"Yes, yes," he said. "Yes?"

"This is Mr. I. Doanwashi, Harold," Peterkin said. "You can call him Doan for short. He's the fella that jumped Parsley Jack. Jack is over to Doc Gravelmeyer's."

"Suspicion of murder," said Harold. He took a big green and gold fountain pen from the desk-set in front of him and wrote in a leather-bound ledger. "Rates are five dollars a day."

"Rates?" Doan repeated.

"Single cell, southern exposure," Peterkin explained. "Home cooking."

"Oh," said Doan. "Will you take a check?"

"On what bank?" Harold demanded.

"The Bank of England."

Harold scowled at him. "Where's that?"

"In England."

Harold nodded. "Oh, I think we can arrange it."

Peterkin said, "Have you got a gun on you?"

"Sure," Doan answered. He pulled the Police Positive out of his waistband and slid it across the desk.

Harold shied back. "Is it loaded?"

"Why, yes. It won't shoot unless it is."

"Take it away!" Harold cried. "Peterkin! You know I've told you I won't have loaded guns around here!"

"I'll keep it," Peterkin soothed, sliding the revolver into his coat pocket. "Well, I got to run along now, Mr. Doanwashi, and see how Parsley Jack is comin'. Harold will show you to your cell. So long."

"So long," Doan answered. He waited until Peterkin had closed the door behind him and then said, "Where's the nearest pawn shop?"

"There's only one—Uncle Ben's Lend-Lease Emporium."

"How much will Uncle Ben give Peterkin on that gun of mine?"

"Just half of whatever he says he did when you come around to redeem it."

"Thanks," said Doan.

Harold stood up. "Right this way, Mr. Doanwashi."

He opened a door at the back of the reception room and preceded Doan into a corridor painted a cool, clean green that glistened quietly in the indirect lighting. Steel bars made an interesting architectural pattern along each wall.

Harold opened a section of bars and said, "Here you are. Dinner hour is over, but I can bring you a late lunch if you want to pay extra for it."

"I've lost my appetite," Doan said.

"Good night," said Harold, closing the barred door.

He went back up the corridor and closed the door into the reception room. Doan looked around. It was a roomy cell, and the cot had a monks' cloth cover on it. The sheets were clean, too. Doan lay down on the cot and stared at the ceiling, and wondered if he was dreaming or if his brain had given way under some unsuspected stress. He decided that in either case it wouldn't do him much good to worry about it, so he went to sleep.

Chapter 7

"HEY! HEY, you!"

Doan rolled over and opened one eye. "What?"

"I'm Dust-Mouth Haggerty. Peterkin said you wanted to see me."

He was standing against the cell door with the bars making parallel grooves in his paunch. He had a round, moon face with a fringe of reddish whiskers and a pug nose that was tilted up at an acute angle. He was wearing what had once been a pair of overalls, and a sheepskin vest and a straw hat with the brim torn off in front, and if Doan hadn't been able to see or hear him, he would still have known he was in the vicinity.

"Oh, yes," said Doan, fanning the air in front of his face with the palm of his hand. "I want to make a deal with you on that ore deposit you discovered. I'm representing the Japanese government."

"What kind of a deal?"

"We want to buy the location."

"For cash money? I don't go for none of that Jap yen-sen confetti."

"Cash money," Doan confirmed. "Gold."

"How much?"

"You name it," Doan said carelessly. "We've got lots of dough, and as soon as we invade the United States and capture Fort Knox, we'll have lots more."

"Hmmm," said Dust-Mouth. "How do I know you are a real Japanese agent? How do I know you ain't some traitor that's just pretendin' he's one?"

"Do you think I'd stay in jail if I had any pull with the United States Government?"

"I dunno," said Dust-Mouth. "Them government men are awful tricky. A fella's liable to find them almost any place. There was even one in the asylum. Went around claimin' he was Hitler, but he didn't fool me."

"Sure not. Where's the claim?"

"It's just—aw, no! We ain't agreed yet."

"Let's get started. Name your asking price."

Dust-Mouth rubbed his chin. "Well, now. I can't hardly until I see what this other fella has to say, on account he really has first call."

"What other fella?" Doan asked.

"The other Jap agent. Do you know him?"

"Could be. What's his name?"

"Pocus."

Doan sat still. "Pocus?" he said at last. "H. Pocus? Hangs out in Hollywood?"

"Yeah."

"He's a character I wouldn't trust too far if I were you. Who told you he was a Jap agent?"

"Oh, I knew that on account of the warrant they got out for him."

"Which they?"

"The government. They're gonna hang him because he's a spy, if they catch him, but of course they won't. I mean, they won't catch him."

"I trust not," said Doan. "How are you going about negotiating with this guy, Pocus?"

"I've got an agent of my own on the job. I figure on getting you and Pocus to bidding against each other"

"That will be very interesting to watch," Doan commented.

The door into the reception room opened suddenly, and Harold's bald head glistened eerily in the light.

"Murder!" he shrieked. "Murder, murder!"

He slammed the door shut again.

"Hey, Harold!" Dust-Mouth called. "Who? Who got murdered? Where?" He lumbered down the corridor and opened the reception room door. "Hey, Harold? Who?" He went on into the reception room and closed the door.

Doan sat on the edge of the cot and held his head in his hands. He sat there for about ten minutes, and then the door opened once more and Harold came slowly and shakily down the corridor and peered gloomily through the bars.

"Murder," he croaked. "Just plain murder."

"Who was the victim," Doan asked, "if you can bear to tell me?"

"Poor old Tonto Charlie. Free-Look Jones went and stabbed him in the neck just because Tonto caught him cheating at cards. Why, that's the nastiest thing Free-Look ever did. A man that'll do a thing like that isn't fit to associate with decent people. You come on out now."

"Why?" Doan asked. "Does this business about Tonto Charlie give everybody a furlough from jail?"

"Oh, no. Parsley Jack got away. He was just faking all the time. When Doc Gravelmeyer gave him the ether, Jack just held his breath, and then when Doe turned around to get a knife, Jack hopped off the operating table and jumped out the window. Doc Gravelmeyer is pretty mad. He says Jack has got no business exerting himself like that because he's got a couple broken ribs."

Doan followed him down the corridor and into the reception room. Harold sat down behind his desk and sighed.

"Murder," he said. "Think of that."

"I am," said Doan. "Thanks for the nap."

"No charge," said Harold. "Good-by."

Doan went out the jail's front door and down the street to the corner. He stopped there and, shading his eyes with the palm of one hand, surveyed the signs along the main street. A block and a half to the south there was a ten-foot tall stretch of red neon tubing that said

BURIALS IN THE BEST OF TASTE
AT REASONABLE RATES
CASH

Doan headed in that direction. The sign ran around and over a nar-

row brick building that had draped, darkened windows on the ground
floor. There was a door beside the windows that was labeled conserva-
tively

DOCTOR ETHELBERT GRAVELMEYER
PHYSICIAN & SURGEON
CORONER
COUNTY SURVEYOR

Opening the door, Doan went up a long, narrow stairway and into
a vintage waiting room that was empty save for some interesting antique chairs and magazines. Another door, at the back, was open, and
Doan went through that into a small office lined with glass-doored cabi-
nets full of ferociously shiny instruments. There was a desk in the corner and a man behind the desk. He had big ears and a bald head and a
long, drooping, houndlike face. He didn't say anything. He didn't move.
He sat still and looked at Doan without much interest.

"Doc Gravelmeyer?" Doan inquired.

The man nodded once slowly.

"I'm Doan," Doan said.

Gravelmeyer nodded again more slowly.

"I came to inquire about a corpse named Tonto Charlie," Doan told
him. "Where is he?"

Gravelmeyer put out one hand and pointed a long yellow forefinger at the floor.

"Downstairs?" Doan asked. "In the undertaking parlor?"

Gravelmeyer nodded.

Doan said, "It's a funny thing about this climate around here.
Corpses deteriorate very rapidly in it. Don't you think so?"

Gravelmeyer shook his head.

"You don't?"

Gravelmeyer shook his head again.

Doan sighed. "Well, how much would you take to think so?"

Gravelmeyer held up his hand with the forefinger pointing up this
time.

"One," said Doan. "One dollar?"

Gravelmeyer raised the hand and the finger.

"Ten?" said Doan.

Gravelmeyer raised again.

"One hundred," said Doan. "And that's where the bidding stops."

Gravelmeyer nodded and dropped his hand on the desk lifelessly.

Doan pointed at the shiny tin alarm clock on Gravelmeyer's desk. "I've been in jail for the last two hours. Tonto Charlie was killed an hour and twenty minutes ago. Right?"

Gravelmeyer turned his hand over, palm up.

"Sure," said Doan. "I haven't got it now, but I'll get it and come back in a minute. Hold everything."

Gravelmeyer smiled.

Doan went out through the waiting room and down the narrow stairs and up the street to the Double-Eagle Hotel. Gerald, the shiny clerk, was still behind the desk in the lobby, and he smiled his nicest.

"Mr. Doanwashi, I'm glad to see you again so soon. There's a telegram here for your friend, Harriet Hathaway."

"Did one come for me?" Doan asked.

"Yes. I gave it to Sheriff Peterkin to deliver to you at the jail."

"Peterkin!" Doan echoed, aghast. "Where's the telegraph office? Quick!"

"On the side street, half a block to your left as you go out the door. It's in the second building."

Doan was on his way. He blew out the front door and down the block, weaving and dodging around startled sightseers. He whirled around the corner, skidded slightly on the turn, and then stopped short.

Peterkin was coming toward him. His head was bent, and he was counting some bills he had in his hand with tenderly absorbed interest.

"I'll take that," Doan said.

"Ah?" said Peterkin, startled. He made an instinctive gesture of concealment. "Oh. What?"

"The money," Doan said.

"Oh," Peterkin said. "The money. You mean—this?"

"That," Doan agreed.

Peterkin sighed and handed him the bills. Doan counted them and then silently held out his hand. Peterkin sighed more deeply and disgorged another twenty-dollar bill. He moistened his lips, watching Doan stow the money in his wallet.

"If you're planning on making an investment," he said, "I could steer you . . ."

"My gun," said Doan.

Peterkin gave it to him. Doan flicked out the cylinder to make sure it was still loaded and then slipped it into his waistband.

"Say," said Peterkin, "did you know that we was both right about Free-Look Jones?"

"How is that?" Doan asked.

"Well, you said he might use his knife if somebody caught him cheatin' at cards, and I said he'd likely run. He did both."

"Where'd he run to?"

"Somewhere or other," Peterkin said vaguely.

"Have you looked for him?"

"Me?" Peterkin said. "Well, no. Not yet. But I'm goin' to as soon as I get around to it. I probably won't find him, though. Say, do you know you parked that big car of yours right smack in the red zone? I hadda give you a ticket."

Doan took a dime out of his pocket and gave it to him.

"Thanks," said Peterkin. "I'll tear that ticket right up."

"Don't bother," Doan told him. "Save it for next time. Have you seen Dust-Mouth Haggerty?"

"Not since he left for Hollywood."

"What?" said Doan. "Hollywood? When did he do that?"

"Oh, a while back."

"Well, why did he do that?"

"He's gonna kill a fella there."

Doan took a deep breath. "He wouldn't, by any chance, be going to kill a guy named Pocus, would he?"

Peterkin looked surprised. "Why, sure. That's it. How'd you know?"

"I wonder myself," said Doan. "What has he got against Pocus?"

"Oh, he's crazy."

"Pocus or Dust-Mouth?"

"Dust-Mouth. I told him that Free-Look Jones was the one that did for Tonto Charlie, but Dust-Mouth claims that Tonto Charlie went to Hollywood to see this Pocus on a deal Tonto Charlie and Dust-Mouth was hatchin' up, and Dust-Mouth says you told him this Pocus wasn't to be trusted, so he thinks Pocus had something to do with Tonto Charlie gettin' killed. He's just crazy, like I said. You can't talk sense to him."

"Did he say when he'd be back?"

"I don't think he will."

"Why not?"

"Say, you should see the stuff the FBI sent out about this Pocus party. They say he's a Jap spy and a gunman and a murderer and a train robber and all kinds of things. I figure that if Dust-Mouth finds him, this Pocus will snaffle him off so fast it'll be funny. I told Dust-Mouth that, but you can't reason with him when he gets up on his ear."

"Good-by, now," said Doan wearily.

He left Peterkin there and went back to the suggestively fiery area illuminated by Doc Gravelmeyer's neon sign. He went in the side door and up the stairs and through the reception room. Everything in the small office, including Doc Gravelmeyer, looked exactly the same as he had left it.

Doan counted out one hundred dollars on the desk. Doc Gravelmeyer smiled and nodded at him in a kindly manner, and Doan went out again.

Carstairs was sitting on the sidewalk right in front of the street door, looking gloomily bored.

"Now don't you give me any trouble," Doan warned. "I've got enough already."

Carstairs merely snorted in contempt.

"Mr. Doan!" Harriet Hathaway screamed. "Oh, Mr. Doan!"

She came running headlong across the street, dodging through the double line of parked cars in its center, and the nearby loungers stopped smoking and/or spitting temporarily and watched with languid interest.

"I've got a telegram!" Harriet panted, waving the yellow envelope crumpled in one hand. "But I can't tell you what it says! But I didn't want to! I mean—Oh, Mr. Doan!"

"Pit it out in papa's hand," Doan advised. "What's the matter?"

Harriet pointed an accusing finger at Carstairs. "It's all his fault—the nasty, dirty thing!"

"What did he do this time?" Doan asked.

"Well, we were in that restaurant, and that theatrical person and her manager—ha! manager, indeed!—insisted on joining Mr. Blue and myself in spite of the fact that it was very obvious we didn't want her to and making sarcastic remarks when I was explaining the Air Force to Mr. Blue, and then he"—her finger stabbed at Carstairs again—"kept walking back and forth under the table and tipping over Mr. Blue's beer and snorting and making nasty sounds!"

"Shame, shame," Doan said to Carstairs.

Carstairs burped at him.

"There!" Harriet cried. "Just like that! Right under the table! And that theatrical person said it was because he wanted to go for a walk! Only she didn't say walk, and she's just nothing but vulgar!"

"Yes," Doan said dreamily. "I mean, isn't she, though? Was there anything else?"

Harriet gasped suddenly. "Oh, yes! I mean, I'm so excited—this telegram…I mean, I got so angry that I just took this awful animal right out of the restaurant and to the hotel, and I was going to lock him in your room! And when I opened the door I saw a duh-duh-duh—"

"Duck?" Doan hazarded.

"No! A dead man!"

Doan groaned. "Oh, no! Not another!"

Harriet gaped at him. "What?"

"A slip of the tongue," Doan said quickly. "This is terrible. Are you sure he was dead?"

"I certainly am! I'll have you know that I graduated at the top of my—"

"Red Cross class in first aid," Doan finished. "Yes, yes. I know. Did you recognize deceased?"

"I think he's that awful little man who sold blondes and brunettes."

"Oh," said Doan in a sick voice. "Just hold still for a minute." He put the palms of his hands against his ears and listened to his brain grind like a rusty cogwheel running around in a rain barrel. He looked up. "All right. Listen closely. Does the name Captain Meredith mean anything to you?"

Harriet opened her mouth and shut it again.

Doan nodded, tapped himself on the chest. "I'm Secret Agent Z-15."

"You!" Harriet said breathlessly.

"In person," Doan agreed. "I had you contacted through headquarters so there wouldn't be any doubt in your mind." He lowered his voice a few dramatic notches. "Are you ready to do, and perhaps die, in the service of your country?"

Harriet stood up straight. "I am."

"Good," said Doan. "Maybe we can arrange it. In the meantime go and sit in the Cadillac. Wait there for me. Take Carstairs with you." He jerked his thumb at Carstairs. "Scram, stupid."

Carstairs eyed him, unmoving.

Doan took a step toward him. "Get!"

Carstairs went, looking back over his shoulder with his upper lip lifted malignantly.

Doan took a deep breath and trudged back up the street and into the lobby of the Double-Eagle.

"Well, good evening!" said Gerald.

Doan didn't bother to answer. He went wearily up the stairs and down the hall. Harriet had used a passkey, and had left it in the lock of the door. Doan opened it, took another deep breath, and looked inside.

The light was on, and Free-Look Jones was laid out neatly on the bed. His hands were folded across his chest, his feet pointed precisely at the ceiling, and he had a knife with a green handle stuck in the side of his throat.

Doan went over and looked at him. He hadn't been mussed up at all. He hadn't even bled on his dapper brown suit or even on the bedspread. His eyes were closed. Doan put his thumb on one of the lids and pushed it open. The pupil of the eye was dilated enormously. Someone had been kind enough to give Free-Look Jones a big slug of morphine before they had operated on him.

Doan went back to the door, looked up and down the hall and listened carefully. After a moment, he took the passkey out of the lock and stepped across the hall to the door opposite and knocked.

The door jerked open, and a red, sullen face peered out at him.

"Well, what?"

"I'm offering a short correspondence course in authorized classics of English Literature—"

"Go away!" the red face snarled. "Shud-up !"

The door slammed emphatically. Doan went to the next one and rapped again. A feminine voice called coyly, "I'm busy right now, dearie."

Doan went on to the next door and tried again. No one answered this time. He rapped again, more loudly. Still he got no results. He tried the passkey in the lock, and it opened at once. He pushed the door open, reached around and flipped the switch.

The room was empty, and the bed was made up. There were no clothes or other odds and ends to indicate that the room had an immediate occupant. Doan went back to his own room and picked up Free-Look Jones as carefully as a mother cradling a baby.

Free-Look Jones wasn't very heavy, and he didn't make any trouble at all as Doan carried him across the hall and deposited him on the bed in the empty room. With his thumb and forefinger, Doan took hold of the green knife handle and pulled the blade free. The skin on Free-Look Jones' neck puckered slightly and then loosened and a few dark drops of blood trickled down on his shirt collar.

The knife looked remarkably like the one that Doan had left appended to Tonto Charlie, and for all he knew it might really be the same one. He was taking no chances. He closed the thin, slanting blade and put the knife in his pocket.

"Nighty-night," he said to Free-Look Jones.

He went out and locked the door. He made another trip into his own room and retrieved the .25 automatic from under the mattress and picked up his suitcases. Carrying them, he went downstairs to the lobby.

"Oh, my," said Gerald. "You're not leaving us so soon?"

"Urgent business," said Doan.

"Well, I hardly feel that we can charge you the full rate for the use of the room for such a short time. Would two dollars be too much?"

"Yes," said Doan. "But here it is. Where's Joshua?"

"Do you want him to carry your bags? I'll call him."

"No. I just forgot to tip him. Where is he?"

"You'll find him in the broom closet at the end of the back hall."

Doan went through the rear door and down a long bare hall. The door at the end of it was ajar, and one of Joshua's feet protruded out of it in a casual fashion.

Doan opened the door wider. Joshua was sitting on the floor, leaning back languorously on a varied assortment of mops that served him for a pillow. He opened his eyes and blinked at Doan without seeing him at all.

"Hi, Joshua," Doan said. "Lend me your pencil, will you? I want to sharpen my knife."

"Sure," said Joshua. He fumbled around in the pockets of his jacket and came up with a stub of pencil.

Doan made a few passes at it with the green handled knife, and then put the pencil in his own pocket and handed the knife to Joshua.

"Thanks," he said.

Joshua put the knife in his pocket. "Think nothing of it, pal. Want a drink of root beer?"

"No," said Doan. "You take one. In fact, maybe you'd better take two."

He went back to the lobby and picked up his suitcases.

"By the way," he said to Gerald, "that Joshua is rather a strange character, isn't he?"

"Quite," said Gerald.

"Do you ever have any—ah—trouble with him?"

"Oh, no."

"I'm a psychologist," Doan said. "I detect certain traits of homicidal nature there. I'd remember that if I were you, if anything should—happen."

Gerald smiled soothingly. "Oh, nothing will happen here."

"That's what you think," said Doan, going out the door.

He lugged the suitcases over to the Cadillac. Harriet was standing beside it, biting her lower lip and making little jerky, angry motions with her clenched fists.

"Now he won't even let me in! He just growls at me!"

Doan opened both a rear and front door. "In front," he said to Carstairs. "And no acts if you don't want a pop in the puss. I'm a busy man at this point."

Carstairs took his time about crawling out of the back seat and into the front. He sat on the floor, with his nose pushed against the windshield and glowered sullenly.

"Can you drive this?" Doan asked Harriet.

"With him in there?"

"He won't bother you. He's sulking now."

"Well, why?"

"He has to associate with me because I own him," Doan explained. "But he picks his own friends."

"But I don't want to sit close to him!"

"Are you refusing an order from your superior officer?" Doan demanded severely.

"Well, no."

"Drive," said Doan.

Harriet gulped bravely. "Well, where?"

"To Hollywood. Wake me up when we get there if I don't die in my sleep, I hope."

Chapter 8

SUNRISE ON THE DESERT IS NOT SO TERRIFIC AS sunset, but it's pretty disconcerting at that when it comes on you unexpectedly. It's awfully bright and enthusiastic in a gruesome way.

"Mr. Doan!"

"Uh?" said Doan. He was tied in a running bowline knot on the back seat. He sat up and looked at the leering bloodshot eye of the sun, and got cramps in both legs and a slight case of *mal de mer* simultaneously.

"Wake up!" Harriet ordered.

"Why?" Doan asked.

"It's going to rain!"

"I don't recall inquiring about the current state of the climate in this hell hole," Doan said, "but just in case I did, what of it?"

"It's against the law!"

"Raining is against the law?" Doan asked.

"No! Telling you it's going to rain is against the law."

"Then why are you doing it?" Doan inquired.

"I just can't understand people who are all blurry and stupid when they wake up. I never am. Of course I didn't mean that my telling you it was going to rain was against the law, but the radio just said it was, and that's against the law. You're not supposed to give out weather conditions in advance. That's a rule laid down by the Defense Command, and it's a very serious offense to violate it."

"All right," said Doan.

"Well, the radio announcer just said it was going to rain. Right out on the air. Suppose a Japanese spy heard him say that? And besides it's not true."

"Sure," said Doan.

"Oh, you're not even listening! Wake up!"

"I'm afraid I'm going to," said Doan. "What's not true?"

"It's not going to rain. It never rains in the desert."

"Is that a fact?"

"Of course it is! The reason the desert is a desert is because it's dry, and the reason it's dry is because—"

"It doesn't rain," Doan finished. "Yes, yes. It all comes back to me now. Where are we?"

"We're coming into Talmuth."

Carstairs put his chin on the back of the front seat, and raised one pricked ear and lowered it, and then raised the other and lowered it, and then raised both and waggled them meaningly.

"Okay," said Doan. "Stop the car, Private Hathaway."

"Why?"

"Because you're going to wish you did if you don't. Carstairs wants to go."

Harriet pulled the car over on the shoulder and stopped. "That dirty thing! He just always has to do something!"

"Ain't it the truth," said Doan, leaning over to unfasten the door for Carstairs. "Out, damned spot, and don't think I'm going to come and supervise you, either."

Carstairs wandered away, sniffing disconsolately at dried brush.

"Mr. Doan," said Harriet, "I think I ought to have had a serious talk with Mr. Blue before I left."

"What about?"

"He didn't know about the war, and I don't believe he'd know about selective service, either. Even if he found out, he'd be too shy to go and register all by himself, don't you think?"

"Yes," said Doan. "I don't think. Did you find out where he lived?"

"On the reservation."

"The what?"

"The reservation. He has to. He's part Indian"

"What brand of Indian?"

"Mohican."

Doan sighed. "Don't tell me that he's the last of the Mohicans."

"Why, yes, he is. That's what makes him so shy. He has no one to talk to on his reservation. I think a person has a duty in a case like that, don't you? I mean, the Indians are wards of the government, you know, and the Government is just nothing less than the people, and the people—"

"Are us," Doan concluded. "Yes, yes." He whistled shrilly between his teeth. "Stupid, snap it up!"

Carstairs came back and crawled into the car.

"No luck?" Doan inquired.

Carstairs grunted.

"Drive on," Doan requested. "Forward. Don't wake me up until you see the whites of my eyes."

Chapter 9

FORENOONS IN SOUTHERN CALIFORNIA ARE wonderful, except when they're not, and in that case there's no use in discussing the matter at all. This one was ordinarily wonderful. The sun was shining and soft breezes were slithering, and there were some small, shy, freshly washed clouds distributed where they would do the least good.

"Mr. Doan!"

"Ahem," said Doan.

"Well, I think it's about time you should wake up! Goodness, it's almost noon! I loathe people who sleep late. I mean, it's not normal, do you think?"

"Ummm," said Doan. "Where are we?"

"In San Fernando Valley. I came that way because there's less traffic. We're just coming to Cahuenga Pass. See?"

"Umm," said Doan. "Where's Carstairs?" He untangled his feet and put them down on what should have been the floor, and Carstairs snarled at him sleepily. "How'd he get in here with me?"

"Well, I put him back there because he was leaning on me and snoring in my ear in a very disgusting way. I don't think people should let dogs ride in cars, anyway."

"Yeah," said Doan. "Take the Cahuenga runway and turn to the left at Sunset."

"Why?" Harriet asked.

"Okay," said Doan. "Turn to the right."

"Well, Mr. Doan, there's no use in getting sarcastic about it, is there? I just wanted to know."

Doan sighed. "I want to go to a drive-in restaurant, and the reason

I want to go there is because I'm hungry, and the reason I'm hungry is because Mr. Blue ate my steak last night."

"You should have gotten another."

"Sure."

They went up and dawn the smooth lift of Cahuenga Pass, and through the underpass, and across Hollywood Boulevard and turned to the left on Sunset.

"Pretty quick now," Doan said. "There it is. Drive on in."

The Cadillac rolled up and stopped under the wooden, pagoda-like awning. The trim little girl in the red pants and the red jacket and the high hussar's hat with the plume in it came out and looked at them and went back inside again. They could see her through the plate glass front of the restaurant. She was arguing with the man behind the cash register. She lost. She came out again.

She slapped a card on the windshield and said, "It would be my luck to be on alone."

"I'm glad to see you again, too," Doan told her. "Do you suppose you could scare up some warm gruel—warm, not hot—all full of cream and junk for poor old Carstairs?"

"Not for a seven-cent tip."

"I'm in the chips now. I'll make it a dime even."

"Four bits."

"I'm bleeding, but it's a deal. What'll you have to eat, Harriet?"

"Make it heavy, honey," said the waitress. "For what you have to put up with, you need strength."

"I don't know what you mean," Harriet said coldly.

"Then I sure pity you. You're going to live but not for long or very well if I'm any judge."

"I'll have an order of hot cakes and coffee," said Harriet. "But are you going to let the dog eat here?"

"We're not any more particular than you are, honey," said the waitress. "What do you want?"

"Same," said Doan.

"And three glasses of water, I suppose"

"Four," said Doan. "Five, counting Harriet's."

"Anything for a gag," said the waitress, going back inside the restaurant.

"She's horribly rude," said Harriet. "I don't see why you didn't go to a better place than this. I don't think it's good policy to eat in cheap places."

"I'm saving the government money."

"Oh, yes!" said Harriet. "I'm sorry. I'd forgotten you had an expense account. I think it's very decent of you to save on it."

"Me, too," said Doan.

The waitress came back with three trays, and gave Doan and Carstairs two in the back seat, and Harriet one in the front. She made an extra trip for the water, and then brought the hot cakes and gruel.

Doan tied into his hotcakes eagerly, pausing only to pour water for Carstairs, and then to shove him off the seat when he tried to climb up on it. He had speared the last portion of hotcake and was carefully mopping up the remains of his syrup with it when Harriet said, "Oh!"

She started the motor, and before Doan could even raise his eyes, she slammed the car into reverse and shot backwards across the graveled lot and straight out into the humming traffic of Sunset Boulevard. Doan cringed. Tires wailed, and horns wapped indignantly from all directions, and then there was a long, lingering, final crunch.

Doan hit the plate on his tray with his face. He straightened up slowly and wiped the syrup out of his eyes with a paper napkin. Carstairs snarled in a manner that indicated that he had had just about enough.

"Double that," said Doan. "Now what—"

Harriet wasn't in the front seat any more. Doan opened the rear door and got out and listened to seven drivers tell him what they thought about things in general.

The Cadillac had traveled clear across the street, and was backed half-up over the opposite parking strip. Doan walked around to the back of it. The Cadillac had pinned another car—a topless, nondescript little roadster—right against the base of a concrete lamp post. It had done the roadster no good, at all.

Blue was standing up in the seat of the roadster, surveying the strips of tin that were pleated neatly fore and aft of him. He didn't seem excited or frightened, just hopeless.

"What did I ever do to you?" he asked Harriet. "Well, I saw you going past," Harriet said, "and I didn't know how to stop you."

"Oh yes, you did," Blue contradicted.

The waitress tapped Doan on the shoulder. "So. Trying to sneak out without paying, and with the trays and dishes, huh? See what happens to people who try to chisel? Let it be a lesson to you."

"All right," said Doan wearily.

"The bill will be one dollar and twenty-one cents—plus four bits"

Doan gave it to her. The waitress tested the coins one after the other with her teeth, and then got the trays and dishes and strutted back across to the restaurant. She went in the door and came right out again. She stuck out her tongue in Doan's direction and made a loud, rude noise.

"And the boss said I could! And he says don't come back!"

They had attracted quite a rooting section by this time, and a policeman came puttering along the boulevard on a blue and chrome scooter, and wheeled around beside them and stopped.

"All right, all right. Now who hit who and why?"

"I hit him," said Harriet. "I wanted to talk to him."

"Talk to me instead," the policeman ordered.

"It's business of a purely private nature," Harriet informed him.

"What do you say?" the policeman asked Blue.

"I can't think of anything," Blue said.

The policeman pointed at the roadster. "Well, what about this?"

"It's my contribution to the scrap metal drive," Blue said. "Tell them to come around and pick it up."

"Oh, that's patriotic!" Harriet exclaimed.

"No, it ain't," said the policeman. "He just thinks he's gonna dodge out of a tow charge, but it don't work."

Harriet snapped around at him. "Are you trying to hinder the war effort?"

"Lady," said the policeman, "do you think it would hinder the war effort if I put you in jail?"

"You wouldn't dare!"

"Just go ahead and dare me, and see," the policeman invited grimly.

"Tweet-tweet," said Doan, holding out a twenty dollar bill between two fingers. "Would this cover the tow charge?"

"Sure," said the policeman, capturing the bill with practiced skill. "And who are you?"

"She's my driver," Doan said, indicating Harriet.

"Man, you sure hold your life cheap," the policeman said. "Now come on, folks. Break it up. Move on. And as for you three playmates, go somewhere else and have fun. I don't want to find you around this district again in the near future."

"I want Mr. Blue to come with us," Harriet said.

"Okay," Doan agreed. "Anything you say, but I drive from here on in."

"Now you're getting half way smart," the policeman told him. "Come on, folks. It's all over. No blood and brains. Move on. Break it up."

Doan boosted Carstairs into the front seat, and slid in under the steering wheel. Blue and Harriet got in the back. There was one last heave and rattle from the roadster as they pulled loose, and then the Cadillac rolled on down Sunset toward Vine.

"Now, Mr. Blue," said Harriet, "I want to talk to you about the draft."

"I don't feel it," Blue said.

"No, no! Not that kind of a draft. It's not really a draft at all. It's selective service, and it's the way the government chooses the men who are to have the honor of serving in our Armed Forces. Are you registered?"

"Nope."

"You aren't! Then you'll have to go and do it right away!"

"Nope."

Harriet gasped. "But why not?"

"I don't wanna."

"You don't want to be in the Army?"

"Nope."

"But why?"

"I don't like war."

"Oh," said Harriet, breathing deeply in relief. "That's just because you don't understand the great issues that are involved in this worldwide conflict between the powers of evil and the forces of freedom. Do you?"

"Nope."

"I'll explain them to you"

Doan turned down Vine Street. "Just a moment before you do. How come you followed us to Los Angeles, Blue?"

"Followed you?" Blue echoed. "I ain't that crazy, Mr. Doan. I came here on business."

"Name it."

"Well, I came to see a doctor."

"Oh, are you sick?" Harriet asked.

"Yup."

"Do you think you're too sick to pass the Army examination?"

"If I ain't, I will be soon," said Blue.

"Now you're just being silly. I'm sure you just don't take care of yourself properly. Do you take deep breathing exercises every morning?"

"Nope."

"You should. I'll show you how."

"All right," Blue said resignedly.

Doan turned off Rossmore, and pulled the Cadillac in at the curb in front of the Orna Apartment Hotel. A round, sleek little man with horn-rimmed glasses and three strands of blue-black hair slicked across the dome of his skull was standing on the steps. He had his hands clasped behind him, and he was teetering up and down on his toes surveying his surroundings with a proud, proprietary smile.

"Mr. Rogan," Doan called.

The bald man's smile curdled. He stared in glazed horror for a split second, and then whirled and dove through the front door.

"Wait here for a moment," Doan told Blue and Harriet. "We'll be back."

He and Carstairs went into the apartment lobby. It was very thoroughly empty. Doan went the length of it to the door next to the back hall that had a neat, enameled plaque saying "Manager" on it.

"Mr. Rogan," Doan said, tapping on the door. "Whoo-hoo, Mr. Rogan."

There was an emphatic silence from behind the door.

"I've come to pay my bill, Mr. Rogan," Doan said.

No answer.

Doan took a twenty-dollar bill from his wallet, folded it lengthwise, and then knelt and thrust the edge of it tantalizingly under the door. Somebody tried to snatch it from the other side, but Doan jerked it back.

"Mr. Rogan," he said.

The bolt snapped, and then the key grated in the lock, and then the door opened just wide enough to show that there was a heavy metal chain holding it from opening farther. One of the lenses of Mr. Rogan's horn-rimmed glasses glittered through the crack.

"You give me my money."

Doan rustled the bill enticingly. "Mr. Rogan, I want to rent my apartment again."

"No!"

"Aw, come on," said Doan. "I'll pay my bill and pay in advance."

"We're full up! We're closed! I'm out of business! Go away!"

"Now, Mr. Rogan, you know what happens to people who tell lies."

"Mr. Pocus, I will not have you in my building. You're a criminal!"

"Oh, no," said Doan. "Not any more. I've changed my character and my business and even my name. My name is Doan now. Don't you think that's an improvement on Pocus?"

"No! Go away!"

Doan looked over his shoulder at Carstairs and said, "Woof."

Carstairs sat down and filled his lungs to capacity, and tilted his head back and bayed. The sound was indescribable. It filled the lobby until the walls bulged, and the echoes whimpered in the corners for minutes after Carstairs had cut off their source

"He can do that all day," Doan said, taking his fingers out of his ears.

The chain rattled, and Mr. Rogan crept cringingly out into the lobby. He was holding his head in both hands.

"Please, Mr. Pocus—I mean, Mr. Doan—why don't you go away?"

"I like you, Mr. Rogan," Doan said. "Carstairs does, too. And we both like your apartment hotel. It's so quiet here. That is, it will be unless you refuse to give me my apartment back again."

"Why do these things happen to me?" Mr. Rogan demanded plaintively. "I'm a good citizen. I'm honest. I'm only trying to earn a living for my three divorced wives." He sighed deeply. "What is this new profession of yours, Mr.—ah—Doan?"

"I just go around looking at things."

"An inspector?" Mr. Rogan inquired.

"You could call it that. I collect things, too."

"What things?" Mr. Rogan asked suspiciously.

"Secrets and stuff."

"You give me your word that it's an honorable profession?"

"Certainly," said Doan. "People in my new line of work are much sought after these days."

"All right," said Mr. Rogan. "But in advance, remember. In advance, strictly. Edmund!"

Very slowly Edmund's curly head rose above the level of the desk. He parked his snub nose on the edge of it and looked from Doan to Carstairs, and then back again.

"Ah, Edmund," said Doan. "And how are you, my boy?"

"Mr. Pocus," said Edmund. "I mean, Mr. Doan, I didn't tell those G-men on you. I really didn't. They asked me if you lived here, and I wouldn't tell them."

"That's very nice of you, Edmund," Doan said. "I'll remind Mr. Rogan to give you a raise. Now you two just ready up the receipts and things, and I'll be back flush in a flash."

He went out to the Cadillac. Harriet had Blue crowded into one corner of the back seat, instructing him in a firm and kindly manner on the latest theories of medicine.

"Private Hathaway," Doan said. "We're going to set up temporary headquarters in a couple of apartments here. Come on in."

"You come, too," said Harriet. "I'm not through yet."

"Yes, ma'am," said Blue glumly.

They went back into the lobby.

"Mr. Rogan," Doan said, "I want you to meet Miss Harriet Hathaway. She works for me. I want to rent an apartment for her, too."

"Oh, no!" said Mr. Rogan. "Strictly, no! None of that sort of thing in my building."

"Just what do you mean by that?" Harriet snapped.

"No goings on," said Mr. Rogan.

"Do you dare to stand there and insult your country's uniform?"

"What?" said Mr. Rogan, dazed.

"Shush-shush," Doan said to Harriet.

"Well! Governmental secrecy or not, no one is going to insinuate that I—Well, indeed! I'll have you know, Mr. Rogan, that I'm doing confidential work for Mr. Doan and that we're the merest acquaintances in private life. We're not emotionally interested in each other in the slightest. Mr. Blue, here, has preempted that position in my heart."

"What?" said Blue hoarsely.

"Well, you know you have. There's no point in being silly and bashful about it."

"Hey!" said Blue.

"Not now. We'll discuss it at some more opportune time, in private."

"Oh," Blue moaned.

Harriet looked Mr. Rogan right in the eye. "Are you going to rent me an apartment so I can continue my work for Mr. Doan, or shall I report you to the authorities as a traitor to your country and a fifth columnist?"

"Excuse me," said Mr. Rogan. "I think I'll go lie down. I don't feel well. Edmund, sign the people up. And remember. In advance, strictly."

Chapter 10

THE BATHTUB IN APARTMENT 229 HAD BEEN cleaned and polished during Doan's absence, and he was sitting in it splashing and splattering contentedly when he felt a draft on the back of his neck.

"Yes," said a voice. "You've got all the soap off."

Doan turned around slowly. Arne was standing in the doorway. Barstow was looking over his shoulder.

"Now don't get in an uproar," Doan said. "I've already been to Heliotrope. I just got back."

"Where's the ore deposit?"

"That's a matter we'll have to go into at great length some time. How about next Tuesday?"

"Here," said Arne, handing him a towel.

Doan sighed, turned the drain lever and got up and dried himself.

"And here," said Arne, handing him the bathrobe.

Doan put it on and followed them into the living room. He sat down on the chesterfield. Arne and Barstow sat down and watched him. There was quite a long silence.

"Where's Carstairs?" Barstow asked at last.

"In his sulking corner," Doan said.

"What's he mad at now?"

"He doesn't like the job you gave me. It involves associating with too many people he disapproves of."

"How does he feel about us, anyway?"

"Hey, you," said Doan.

Carstairs' head appeared very slowly above the back of the chesterfield.

"Look who's come to see us," Doan invited.

Carstairs studied Arne and Barstow thoughtfully for about thirty seconds, and then he yawned in a very elaborate manner and pulled his head down out of sight.

"I get it," said Barstow.

"Don't feel hurt," Doan advised. "You should have seen the way he looked when I introduced him to a senator once."

"Let's stop the clowning," Arne said. "Doan, what was the idea of going around telling everybody that you were a Japanese spy? All this cute stuff about I. Doanwashi and the rest of it?"

"You told me Dust-Mouth Haggerty was a whack. When you're dealing with a whack you have to act whacky. If you act normal, he'll think you're on the offbeat. I didn't know how much trouble I'd have finding him, and I was just laying sort of a ground fire."

"It spoiled all the buildup we gave you under the name of Pocus. We expected you to keep on using that name. Why did you take it in the first place?"

"On account of his fans," Doan said, jerking his thumb toward the back of the chesterfield.

"What fans? Why does he have fans?"

"He trains dogs for the Army. He's been making some movie shorts about how it's done, and all such. They show those not only to soldiers but to dog owners, and then the owners pester the Army until they find out who he is, and then they come around and make goo on him. He'll take only very small doses of goo before he takes a leg back in trade. I got tired of trying to keep him from assassinating fat ladies and cute little tots, so I decided to be H. Pocus and assistant."

"That's what you should have stayed. We put out the buildup about Pocus in Heliotrope because we knew Dust-Mouth hung around the jail there and would pick it up from Peterkin."

"Why not from Harold?" Doan asked.

"Who?"

"Harold. The majordomo of the jail."

"What about him?" Arne inquired coldly.

"Nothing," said Doan. "Only I thought he'd spread the news to Dust-Mouth on account he's FBI"

"How did you know that?"

Doan shrugged. "All private detectives can spot a government man—if they stay in business long. When are you going to pounce on Peterkin and Gravelmeyer and Heliotrope in general?"

"The indictments are all ready now, but we're frying bigger fish first. So let's get at it. You contacted Dust-Mouth. What happened?"

"I convinced him," said Doan. "We'll make a deal as soon as I can find him."

"He'll find you. He'll call you here."

"How do you know?" Doan asked.

"We arranged it."

"Come, come," said Doan. "We're not in a B picture—yet. I'd just as soon know how you arranged it."

Arne said, "I suppose I'd better tell you or you'll butch this all up too. Ever hear of Gower Gulch?"

"You mean the place where all the horse opera cowboys hang out?"

"Yes. Most of them are the genuine article, outside of a few professional rodeo and circus performers. Every Western picture has a few old prospectors and desert rats and such kicking around in it for atmosphere. They're mostly genuine, too. They all hang out together, and Dust-Mouth knows lots of them. We put out the rumor that it would be a profitable idea for him to call you here. We used the name Doan this time. Dust-Mouth will be certain to see some of the boys from Gower Gulch if he comes to town, and they'll relay the information."

"Dust-Mouth has sort of a down on Pocus," Doan said. "Maybe he'll spend his time hunting him instead of calling Doan."

"No. There's a new bulletin about Pocus circulating in Gower Gulch. He's just been shot while he was trying to blow up an airplane factory."

Doan sighed. "Things certainly move fast these days. Sorry to hear about old Pocus. He was a fine chap."

"He concealed it well, though," Arne said. "Now there's another little matter. Just what happened to Tonto Charlie?"

"Who?" said Doan.

"You heard me."

"Yes. But the name's not familiar at all."

"Isn't it? He was sort of a weird character who used to make his living by taking money for smuggling aliens across the line in the desert. We've never been able to get a grip on him because he never actually did it. He used to take the aliens out in the desert south of the line in Mexico and lose them there. Sometimes they didn't die. It didn't make any difference to Tonto Charlie because he got half his dough in advance, and that's all he wanted. He's been having a tough time since the war because we're hand-in-hand with the Mexican patrols now."

"He sounds like a delightful character," Doan commented. "But I still don't know him."

"Dust-Mouth Haggerty sent him here to contact Pocus. Did you see him? You'd better think about your answer."

"Never saw him in his life," said Doan solemnly.

"He turned up dead in Heliotrope. He wasn't killed there. Someone killed him somewhere else and brought him there."

"How strange," said Doan. "But then, of course a man like that would have a lot of enemies. Desperate people, no doubt."

"No doubt," Arne agreed. "A man named Free-Look Jones was accused of killing him."

"Jones," Doan repeated thoughtfully. "Free-Look Jones . . . Oh, yes. I thought the name was familiar. He's that strange person who jumped out the window when I offered to buy him a beer."

"He threw a knife at you before he jumped."

"That was just horseplay," Doan said. "You know how people pull gags in bars just to pass the time away. I thought nothing of it. So he killed Tonto Charlie. Tsk, tsk. I hope he has been apprehended and is on his way to his just and proper punishment?"

"He's dead. Did you ever study medicine?"

"No."

"Art?"

"No."

"Anatomy?"

"Well, yes."

"Where?"

"Oh, on the street on windy days, and at the beaches and at the burlesque shows . . . Well, do you want all the details of my private life?"

"This isn't funny," said Arne. "And neither are you. Jones was killed by someone who knew quite a lot about how to operate on a jugular vein so it would drain down into the victim's lungs instead of spurting around."

Doan cringed. "Ghastly. Let's talk about something else."

"All right. What's the idea of the girl named Hathaway in the apartment down the hall?"

"My secretary," said Doan. "And you needn't look that way about it. You've got a secretary, haven't you?"

"Who's the guy with the beard and the black cheaters?"

"Her secretary. There's an awful lot of detail work in this spying business."

Arne watched him in silence for a moment. "You're fast on your feet, but just remember that we've got a long arm and we're awfully long winded."

"You're telling me," said Doan.

Arne stood up. "We won't bore you any more but—"

The telephone buzzed softly.

"Answer that," Arne ordered. "I think it may be Dust-Mouth. Don't drop this one on the floor, or you'll scare him off permanently."

Doan picked up the telephone. "Yes?"

The voice came in a hoarse whisper: "Is this a fella named Doan?"

"That's right."

"Where was you last night?"

"In jail in Heliotrope."

"Who'd you see there?"

"You."

"Uh!" said the voice. It breathed hoarsely for a moment. "Hickey's Wickiup. Eleven-thirty. Say 'Diamond Hitch' to the bull fiddler."

"Right," said Doan.

The line clicked and was dead.

Doan put the telephone down and turned around. "I got him. I'm to be passed on from a joint called Hickey's Wickiup. Now listen. You must have hauled me in this for some good reason, but I'm tired of meeting you every time I take a bath. Why don't you go sit down in some quiet corner and let me sneak up on Dust-Mouth?"

"Okay," said Arne. "Come on, Barstow, we'll move along."

Barstow paused in the doorway. "We'll give you plenty of rope." He made a suggestive circle around his neck with his forefinger and closed the door.

"Funny mans," Doan said sourly. "Hey, you."

Carstairs' head appeared slowly above the chesterfield.

"Did you ever think of what a decoy duck must feel like when it's sitting there waiting for somebody to shoot over its head?" Doan asked.

Carstairs stared at him unwinkingly.

"Never mind," said Doan. "I know now."

Chapter 11

HICKEY'S WICKIUP WAS NOT SO EASY TO find, but Doan finally ran it down in an alley off Gower, north of Sunset. There was nothing special about the alley, except that it was narrow and dark. Doan parked the Cadillac a half block up the street and got out.

"You stay here," he said to Carstairs. "If you see any G-men around you have my permission to bark or even to bite them."

Carstairs watched him suspiciously.

"Only one beer," Doan promised. "On my word of honor."

Carstairs sighed resignedly, and lay down on the seat. Doan went back to the alley and felt his way along it cautiously. At the back it widened out, and he groped around in the gloom until he hit a wooden gate that swung back smoothly under his hand. A cowbell went bing-bong in a flat, discouraged tone somewhere ahead.

Doan headed in that direction, and suddenly a door opened wide in front of him. A fat man wearing a purple silk shirt and enormous handle-bar mustaches beamed at him and bellowed enthusiastically

"Howdy there, stranger. Welcome to Hickey's. Light and set."

"Thanks, pardner," Doan answered. "Reckon I will."

He squeezed through the door into a low, smoky room that had all the trimmings, even to the smell of horse sweat from the saddle blankets strung over the rafters. The back of a chuck wagon had been built into the rear wall. The range cook, complete with peaked sombrero and leather brush-scarred chaps, squatted in front of it, manipulating frying pans and iron pots with offhand skill, over an open charcoal fire that had a protective hood to suck up the fumes. Several other characters in cowboy outfits lounged or squatted around him, consuming the results of his efforts. The tables around the room were made of split logs, and the chairs of nail kegs.

There were quite a few people here. They were mostly men, and all in some kind of western dress, from a hundred percent to a pair of hand made boots. There were some women, and Doan recognized a serial queen who was wearing a chinchilla coat over a pair of blue jeans. The bar was made out of plain pine planks, and Doan shoved up against it and said, "Beer."

The bartender looked like an aged and dilapidated version of one of the Dead End Kids. "Dime," he said, slapping the glass down. "You an agent?"

"Agent?" Doan repeated.

"Picture agent?"

"Nope," said Doan. "Tenderfoot."

"Huh!" said the bartender, and went away.

The orchestra started to play in an aimless way. It consisted of a regular fiddle, a bull fiddle and an accordion, and it was not so bad, either. They played a roundelay that Doan had never heard before. He sipped his beer, waiting, and when they had finished crossed the room to their platform and held out a folded dollar bill toward the bull fiddle player.

"Can you play Diamond Hitch?" he asked.

"Sure thing," said the bull fiddle player. He took the dollar bill leaving a small slip of paper in Doan's palm.

Doan went back to the bar and finished his drink and then walked to the door.

"You ain't a-leavin' us so soon, are you, stranger?" the fat man asked.

"Yup," said Doan. "Gotta go home and shear my sheep."

"Drop in again, stranger. We don't even bar sheepherders here, not unless they start to bleatin'."

Doan went through the gate, causing the cowbell to bing-bong dolorously again, and then down the alley to the street and up the block to the Cadillac.

"See?" he said to Carstairs. "Only one beer, just like I said."

Carstairs grunted and moved over on the seat. Doan slid in under the wheel and snapped on the dashlight. He unfolded the slip of paper. Printed on it in pencil were the words

OLD LISTON LOT COME
PEARL ST ENTRANCE

"Okay," said Doan.

Chapter 12

AWAY BACK BEFORE YOU CAN REMEMBER they made silent motion pictures. This, of course, was too good a thing to last long, and, sure enough, some evil genius cooked up the idea of assaulting your ears as well as your eyes. Everybody took to it with, literally, a whoop and a holler, but the casualties in the business were spectacular, and among the first and the sorriest were the sets that had been used formerly for outdoor shots. Everything was sound staged now, and these veterans of many a catsup-blood battle were retired to odd way-points, like the Liston Lot, and left there to contemplate their celluloid sins.

The Liston Lot in prehistoric times had actually been a place where they shot pictures, and it was still surrounded by a twenty-foot wall that had looked sternly forbidding in its day, but which time and the weather had revealed to be nothing but stucco, plastered over lath and chicken wire. It was dark and forbidding as the mad scientist's castle, as Doan idled the Cadillac along Pearl Street and parked opposite the niche that marked the side gate.

There was not a light showing. Doan got out of the car and jerked his head at Carstairs. Their shadows joggled eerily ahead of them, and Doan's heels clicked in empty, fading cadence as they crossed the pavement. The iron-barred gate was closed, but when Doan pushed at it, it swung back with a rusty mutter of hinges.

Inside Doan could only see the vague, grotesque jumble of half-buildings, piled together like the results of a bad bombing raid. No guard or caretaker was visible. Doan whistled once softly. A breeze moved stealthily past his face and rattled a piece of lath against some boarding, but there was no other sound or movement.

Carstairs nudged his head against Doan's thigh, and when Doan looked down at him, he swung around to peer with pricked ears down a ragged, straggling side lane where the dim light caught and gleamed back from the scummed surface of a ten-foot puddle of water.

"That you, Dust-Mouth?" Doan inquired.

A shadow moved and thickened. "Who's there?"

"Well, now guess," said Doan.

"Doanwashi?"

"You're sharp tonight. Do you want to go on playing hide and seek, or did you have something else in mind?"

"I'm scared."

"We won't let the bad mans hurt you," Doan said.

"We! Who you got with you?"

"My dog."

Dust-Mouth's breath made a tiny whistle. "Dog! Pocus had a dog!"

"Sure," said Doan. "I inherited him when Pocus got blown up. He helps me spy now."

"Pocus got shot, not blowed up!"

"Shot—blown up—what's the difference to him?" Doan asked indifferently. "Or you?"

"I'm scared."

"So we're back there again, are we? What shall I do about it, shiver for you?"

Dust-Mouth gulped. "Well—well, you still want to make that deal?"

"Certainly," said Doan.

"Come on back this way, then."

Doan circled carefully around the pond, feeling the mud squash queasily under his shoes. Carstairs drifted behind him, lifting his feet daintily.

"Through here," Dust-Mouth directed.

Doan couldn't see him any better, but now he could smell him. Dust-Mouth had accumulated a new aroma to blend with the old ones, and it took Doan a moment to identify it as secondhand wine.

He slid in under a pair of deserted stairs that went nowhere in particular, and then a door creaked and let out a flicker of faint light.

"My hideout," said Dust-Mouth.

There was a lantern sitting on a broken crate, and the light that worked its way out of the grimed chimney revealed the ruin of what had once been a siren's boudoir, featuring a faded green and gilt couch big enough for Cleopatra, and a dresser with a broken mirror and some odd broken-down chairs, plus a piano bench with a lath for a substitute leg.

"Shut the door," Dust-Mouth said.

Doan shut it, and the aroma of wine became so intensified that Carstairs made little grumbling sounds to himself. Dust-Mouth settled down warily on the piano bench.

"I'm scared."

"You told me—remember? What are you scared of? After all, you're only selling out to the enemy in time of war. That's nothing to worry about."

"I don't know," Dust-Mouth said doubtfully. "It don't look so good to me no more. I mean, Tonto Charlie gettin' killed . . . That had a kind of funny effect on me. I was mad at first, and then I got to thinkin'. A fella can't spend no money when he's dead, you know."

"I hadn't thought of it," Doan said, "but I believe you're right. Why don't you have a drink?"

"Drink?"

"Of wine."

"'Ain't a bad idea." Dust-Mouth groped around under the piano bench. "You want some? Here's a cup for you."

It wasn't a cup. It was a horn—evidently a prop for some Viking drinking scene. Doan looked in it, expecting to find at least a spider lurking around somewhere, but it was only slightly dusty. He blew in it and then said:

"Okay."

Dust-Mouth poured wine out of a glass gallon jug. "This here's port. It ain't as good as sherry, but it's better than nothin'."

"I guess so," Doan agreed.

"Here's how," Dust-Mouth said. He raised the jug expertly on his forearm, and wine gurgled.

Doan tasted his, and Carstairs growled at him.

"This is strictly business," Doan said. "Believe me."

"Glum," said Dust-Mouth, lowering the jug at last. "What say?"

"How about my ore location?" Doan asked.

"I got it all right," said Dust-Mouth. He groped around in his overall pocket and extended a cupped, incredibly dirty hand. "Samples."

Doan got as close as he dared, and saw a drift of shiny particles hidden among the other visible debris.

"That there," said Dust-Mouth. "That right there will win the war for you. It's carbo-carbo-bezra . . . It's the stuff. You can look it up, and then take it to an assayer and ask him if it ain't. And do I know where there's plenty of it! Man, you can scoop it up with a steam shovel. Ain't more'n eighteen inches below surface. Millions of cubic yards. Pure."

"Where is it?" Doan asked.

Dust-Mouth looked all around him cautiously and tilted his head to listen with a sort of groggy concentration. The set had been provided with no windows, but whoever had made a hidey-hole out of it by nailing in a back wall had left a gap in the rough boards about two feet square. It was covered with a mildewed piece of burlap.

"Now we got to talk serious," said Dust-Mouth. "Now we got to strike us a deal. Pull up a little closer."

"I like it here," said Doan. "Go ahead."

"Doanwashi, this is gonna be hard for you to believe, but I'm tired of the desert. Fact. I'm just durned tired of dust and cactus and Gila monsters and all such. I crave to see rivers and creeks and green grass and corn growin' in rows. You ever consider what a purty sight corn is when it grows in rows?"

"I like it better in bottles."

"It ain't bad there, neither," Dust-Mouth admitted. "But what I mean is—I gotta admit it—I wanna go back where I come from and set. I wanta go back to Ioway."

"It's still there," Doan told him.

"You Japs figurin' on conquerin' it?"

"Oh, sure. We'll go through that way on the way to Washington."

"What you gonna do with the people?"

"Kill 'em."

"All of 'em?"

"Oh, we'll leave a few. Have to have somebody to spit on when we feel mean."

"I'll tell you what I figure. I want some of that Ioway land. I figure it'd be nice to have a belt of it runnin' along the Mississippi from about Davenport up to about Clinton and about a hundred miles deep. That'd give me plenty of room to move around in, and I could use the river if I got tired of travelin' on the roads. I'd have to have some people to farm it, too, of course. I ain't gonna work."

"Naturally not," Doan agreed. "I guess we could arrange for you to have some peons."

"What's them?"

"Slaves."

"You mean, I wouldn't even have to pay 'em?"

"No."

"Man, you're makin' this sound like the stuff to me. Just think of me sittin' there like a king…Could you arrange that for sure, Doanwashi?"

"Right. If this ore deposit is what you say it is. Otherwise we won't even give you ten acres of Texas."

"It's there! There's a million tons of it!"

"Okay. It's a deal. Where's the ore deposit?"

"We got to shake hands first," Dust-Mouth specified cagily.

Doan took a deep breath and held it. "Okay."

"Now we got to drink on it."

Doan let his breath out and sighed. "Okay."

He raised his horn, and Dust-Mouth tipped the jug up on his forearm. The burlap sacking over the back window ripped with a little soggy sound, and in the same split second there was a sharp, smacking report.

The bullet hit the jug of wine and shattered it, and the whole of its contents cascaded down over the lantern. That was too much for the lantern. It went out with a weary gulp, and the darkness moved into the room in a sudden, silent rush.

Dust-Mouth screamed like a lost soul. Doan was up and on his way to the door, the Police Positive ready in his hand. He tripped and fell into the dresser and broke more of the mirror, and then Carstairs snorted, and he followed the sound to the door.

"Right," he said, nudging Carstairs on that side with his knees.

He pulled the door open and dodged to the left. Carstairs faded away in the other direction. Doan fought his way clear of the stairs and staggered into the side of a thatch-covered hut that collapsed with a soggy puff. He stepped over and through the hut, caromed off the edge of a platform, and then was in the open.

"Hi!" he said.

Carstairs' voice bellowed in answer. Instantly there were two more shots. Doan swore loudly and ran straight ahead. He slammed head on into a brick wall that gave way with a tearing crash.

"Hi!" he yelled.

Carstairs bayed. There was another shot. Doan saw the dim, sprayed flash of it this time and fired back, shooting high. The bullet hit something and snapped off into the air with an angry *wheee.*

A door made a hollow thump. Carstairs bayed angrily.

Doan plowed into another brick wall and went through it like Superman, spraying balsa bricks in all directions. Knee-high weeds clutched at him chummily, and he dodged under a hitching rack and rattled the length of a boardwalk. He whirled around the corner of a saloon front and came face to face with a decayed colonial mansion.

Carstairs was on the veranda with both front feet against the closed front door.

"Go around, you fool!" Doan shouted. "There's nothing behind it! It's a set! Left! Left! Hike!"

Carstairs' claws skittered on the porch, and he leaped over the railing at the porch edge and disappeared again. Doan ran the other way. The colonial mansion was edged cozily in against the front half of a yacht, and Doan squeezed in between them, breaking the yacht's anchor chain in the process.

"Hi!" he called.

Carstairs bayed straight ahead. Doan ran along the narrow street of an early English village, detoured around an igloo, and came out on the corner of Broadway and 42nd Street. He paused, blowing, and the iron side gate clanged to his right.

Doan went that way fast. He found Carstairs with his head stuck between the bars, peering vainly out and down the street.

"Get away," said Doan, pulling him back.

The gate opened inward, and Doan jerked at it. It was locked. Doan swore eloquently. He dropped his revolver in his pocket, took hold of two of the iron bars and heaved back. The lock didn't give, but the hinges did. They pulled loose with a shriek of tortured lath, and Doan went down with the gate on top of him.

Carstairs hopped nimbly through the opening and raced down the street. Still swearing, Doan crawled out from under the gate and went out into the street. There was nothing in sight but the Cadillac. Doan sat down on the curb, holding his revolver in his lap, and waited.

In about five minutes Carstairs came ambling out of the shadows and shook himself in a distasteful way.

"It's a damned shame you aren't a bloodhound," Doan told him. "I've got a notion to trade you in on one."

Carstairs merely looked at him.

"I wasn't so hot, either," Doan admitted. "Let's go pick up Dust-Mouth. He's probably having a katzenjammer all by himself in the dark."

They went back through the wrecked gate and down the lane around the mud puddle. Doan leaned under the stairs.

"Hey, Dust-Mouth. The enemy retired to a previously prepared position."

No one answered.

Doan went into the hideout. "Dust-Mouth."

The scent of wine was overwhelming. Doan took a match from his pocket and snapped it on his thumbnail. The sudden spurt of flame reflected gorily from the spilled wine and the pieces of shattered jug, but there was no sign of Dust-Mouth.

"Hey!" Doan yelled.

The echoes came back sullenly—alone.

"Oh, hell," said Doan.

Chapter 13

EDMUND WAS BEHIND THE DESK WHEN Doan and Carstairs came into the lobby of the apartment hotel. He was working on a new radio diagram.

"A dame called you, Mr. Doan," he said. "I mean, a lady. I mean, she sounded pretty good to me."

"Did she have a name?" Doan asked.

"I guess so, but she didn't tell me what it was. She called you twice, and she said she'd call you back some more. She said it was important."

"Okay," Doan said. "I'll be home for awhile."

"Mr. Doan!" said Harriet.

She came in the front door, her eyes sparkling with eager energy. Blue trailed along disconsolately behind her.

"Have a nice ride?" Doan asked casually.

"Oh, we didn't ride. We walked. It was just wonderful. Wasn't it?"

"I'm tired," Blue said.

"Certainly, but it's a healthy tiredness. It's good for you to feel that way."

"My feet hurt"

"They'll get used to it. Just think of all the hardships our poor soldier-boys are standing all over the world."

"I am," Blue said drearily. He nodded at Edmund. "Get me a taxi, will you?"

Harriet shook her finger at him. "Now you couldn't get a taxi in Africa or the South Sea Islands, you know."

"He probably can't get one here, either," Edmund told her. "But I'll try." He plugged in on the switchboard and dialed expertly.

"Where are you staying, Blue?" Doan asked.

"At the Clark Hotel."

"I'll call you the first thing in the morning," Harriet said. "Now you may kiss me good-night."

"Right here?" said Blue.

"Of course, silly. Edmund and Mr. Doan don't mind."

"I should say not," Doan agreed. "We'll find it very interesting."

Harriet put her cheek up, and Blue pecked at it warily. The effort completed his exhaustion. He backed up and sat down on a divan with a weary sigh.

"Tomorrow morning, remember," Harriet said. "Bright and early."

"Yeah," Blue answered hopelessly.

Edmund said, "The taxi company says maybe they'll send a cab and maybe they won't, depending on how they feel about it."

"I'll wait," said Blue.

"Good-night, dear," Harriet said. "Sleep tight."

"Yeah," said Blue.

Harriet tripped up the stairs, and Doan and Carstairs followed her. She was waiting for them at the top.

"Mr. Doan, I haven't really done any work for you. I really don't feel that I'm doing my bit."

"You're doing just fine," Doan told her. "Carry on. Chin up. Good-night."

"Good-night, Mr. Doan."

Harriet went into her apartment, and Doan went on down the hall toward his. He was feeling for his key when Carstairs approached the door, put his nose against the crack under it, and sniffed once.

"Visitors?" Doan inquired.

Carstairs yawned.

"The Gold Dust twins," Doan said in a disgusted voice.

He opened the door. Arne was sitting in a chair facing it, and Barstow was lying on the chesterfield with his hat over his eyes.

"Well," said Arne, "where is it?"

"I don't know."

"What happened this time?"

"Somebody shot at Dust-Mouth and scared him green."

Arne stood up quickly. "Who?"

"That's the sixty-four dollar question."

"Didn't you see him?"

"No. I chased him, but he was too fast on his feet."

"Did he hurt Dust-Mouth?"

"No. And I'd just made him a present of part of Iowa, so I think he'll probably call me up again when he gets through shaking."

Arne breathed hard through his nostrils. "Probably! That's not good enough. We stayed out of the way. We gave you a clear channel. And now look. A fine thing! And you're supposed to be a smart operator!"

"Fire me," Doan suggested.

"We can do better than that," Arne said. "Or worse. You gave the knife that killed Free-Look Jones to the bellboy, by name of Joshua, in the Double-Eagle Hotel in Heliotrope."

"Did I?" said Doan.

Arne stared at him. "Haven't you any conscience at all? Did you want to get that poor devil convicted of murder?"

"We must all serve our country as best we can in these grim times," Doan said. "Is he? Going to be convicted of murder, I mean?"

"No. He has a perfect alibi. He was making root beer in the drugstore next to the hotel. He put some ether in it, and it knocked him cold. He couldn't possibly have been running around loose at the time Free-Look was killed. He couldn't navigate at all. The druggist carried him over and dumped him in the broom closet. Now they're looking for you."

"I thought they would be," Doan admitted. "But of course the government will protect me from being charged with any minor misdemeanors like murder."

"Ha-ha," said Arne.

Doan nodded. "Why don't you two go home and get a good night's rest?"

"We'll give you twenty-four hours more," Arne said. "Come on, Barstow."

"What happens after twenty-four hours?" Doan asked.

Barstow looked back from the doorway. "You were wrong before. *That's* the sixty-four dollar question. Cheer-o." He closed the door softly.

"I've got a good mind to write a letter to President Roosevelt," Doan said to Carstairs.

He sat down on the chesterfield and took off his shoes. He slid the Police Positive under the cushions, and then lay down on his back and stared gloomily at the ceiling. Carstairs stared at the ceiling, too, and then wearied of it and went to sleep in the middle of the floor.

Someone knocked gently on the door.

"What now?" Doan said, not moving.

The door opened, and Harriet looked in.

"Mr. Doan, I forgot to ask you. Did you take care of the matter of that dead man who was in your hotel room?"

"Oh my, yes," Doan said. "I managed things in my customarily brilliant manner."

"Well, why was he killed?"

"That's a military secret."

"Oh, I see. I don't suppose you can tell me who killed him, either?"

"I don't suppose I can," Doan agreed glumly. "You don't know how I wish I could."

"That's all right, Mr. Doan. I can stand the suspense."

"Yeah," said Doan. "But can I?"

The telephone buzzed.

"Ah-ha!" Doan exclaimed, jumping up off the chesterfield. He picked the instrument up. "Yes?"

"This is Edmund, Mr. Doan. At the desk. Woo-woo!"

"What?" said Doan.

"Oh boy! Wow! Whee! You got a visitor. Have you got a visitor! Mr. Doan, it's Susan Sally, and she wants to see you! Woo-woo!"

"Woo-woo!" said Doan. "Send her right up!"

He dove for the chesterfield and got hastily back into his shoes. He slicked his hair down and straightened his tie.

"What is it?" Harriet asked, startled. "Is something going to happen?"

"Probably not," Doan told her. "But you can't blame me for hoping."

Harriet watched him suspiciously. "Is it that theatrical person?"

"How did you know?" Doan demanded.

Harriet nodded slowly and meaningly. "I thought so. She said she thought you were a very interesting person. I knew what that meant."

"What?" Doan inquired.

"I knew she'd try to see you again. Do you want me to tell her you're busy or not here or something?"

Doan's mouth dropped open. "What?" he repeated incredulously.

"She's not the sort of person you should associate with when you're performing a dangerous and vital mission for your country. I don't approve of her at all."

"Your ballot is void," said Doan. "Would you mind running home and knitting yourself a muffler?"

"You're not going to see her alone? In your apartment? At night?"

"I certainly am," said Doan. "And that reminds me." He nudged Carstairs with the toe of his shoe. "Get. Go with the nice lady."

Carstairs sat up and glared at him in outraged protest.

Someone stumbled in the hall. Doan pushed Harriet aside and opened the door wide. Susan Sally was leaning against the wall opposite, and her eyes were glazed, and she was swaying a little.

"They got me, toots," she said. The muscles in her soft throat tightened suddenly, and the expression on her face changed to one of incredulous, shocked surprise. "Doan!" She coughed. The sound was deep and bubbling in her throat, and then she put out one hand gropingly in front of her and fell forward in a graceful, limp whirl.

Doan caught her before she hit the floor. He stiffened, holding her, staring over her shoulder. On the wall, where she had rubbed against it, there was a wet, red smear.

"What—" said Harriet, scared. "What—"

"Shut-up," said Doan. "Take care of her."

He flicked the .25 automatic out of the breast pocket of his coat and ran down the hall. The self-operating elevator was up at this floor, its door open. Doan went down the stairs three at a time.

Edmund was contemplating his radio diagram with a slap-happy expression on his face. He looked up and saw Doan and the automatic, and came to with a startled gulp.

"Who was with Susan Sally?" Doan asked tightly.

Edmund made stiff mouthing motions and shook his head mutely and helplessly.

"Who came in after her?"

"No—no—no—" Edmund said, doing a little better.

"Who was in the lobby when she came?"

Edmund's face was paper-white. He pointed to himself.

"No one else?"

"N-no," said Edmund. "She ain't m-mad, is she? I didn't do nothin'. I juh-juh-just asked her for an autograph, is all."

"Didn't you notice anything the matter with her?"

Edmund swallowed hard. "I thought maybe she was a little drunk. I mean, she staggered. Not much, though."

"What'd she say when you asked her for an autograph?"

"She just said she was in a hurry now, and she'd give me one when she came out."

"Did she use the elevator?"

"Yes. I told her the stairs were quicker, but she said she couldn't make it. That's what she said. 'I can't make it, bub'. So I thought that was why she was drunk. I mean—staggering and—and that..."

"Where are those damned G-men hanging out?"

"D-down in the garage in the janitor's apartment, but I'm not s-supposed to tell anybody..."

"You tell them to get up to my apartment. Now."

"Yes, sir!" said Edmund, plugging in hastily on the switchboard.

Doan ran back up the stairs. Susan Sally was no longer lying in the hall, and he trotted quickly down it to his apartment and pushed the door open.

Harriet stood up beside the chesterfield. There was blood on her hands, and her face was greenish.

"They never taught me anything like this . . . I—I think she's . . ."

Susan Sally was lying face down on the chesterfield. Harriet had taken off her jacket and blouse. There was a little jagged tear, no wider than a man's thumbnail in the softly tanned skin of her back, left of her backbone, just under her shoulderblade. Dark blood made a thin scribble down toward the hollow of her back.

Doan picked up one hand and felt for the pulse in the wrist. There was none. He pressed his fingers against the side of her neck. Then, very gently, he turned her head sideways and lifted the lid of one eye.

Harriet gulped.

"She's dead," Doan said tonelessly.

Arne came in the room and stopped short. He looked from Susan

Sally to Harriet to Doan. He didn't say anything.

"She was coming to see me," Doan said in the same toneless voice. "Somebody didn't want her to."

Arne touched the flesh around the wound on Susan Sally's back with quick, impersonal fingers. "This is another job by the same one who operated on Free-Look Jones."

"I know!" Harriet cried suddenly. "Oh, I know! Her manager! That's the one! His name is MacAdoo! He did it because he was jealous of her going to see Mr. Doan!"

"What?" said Arne blankly.

"He did! He's a nasty little man! He knew Mr. Doan would win her away from him!"

Arne looked at Doan.

Doan shrugged. "She goes on like that all the time."

"Well, I'm right!" Harriet shrilled. "Of course I'm right! He just couldn't stand the thought of her being interested in anyone else, and so he stabbed her!"

"Elmer A. MacAdoo is the name," Doan said. "In case you're interested."

Arne picked up the telephone. "Janitor," he said when Edmund answered. After a moment he cupped his hand over his mouth and talked in an inaudible voice at some length.

He waited, then. The silence in the room grew and expanded like a living thing. Carstairs stirred uneasily on the floor. Doan looked at him, and he became quiet again.

"Yes," Arne said into the telephone. He listened for a moment and then turned to Doan. "This MacAdoo lives at Malibu Beach. That's about thirty-five miles from here. He's at home. This is supposed to be he on the extension now. See if it is."

Doan took the telephone. MacAdoo's voice was saying angrily, "Hello, hello! Operator! Who is calling? Is this New York? Hello!"

"This is Doan, MacAdoo," Doan said.

"Who? Who did you say?"

"Doan. You met me in Heliotrope."

"Oh! Mr. Doan. Yes. What is it?"

"Susan Sally is here."

"What? She is? Why, she hasn't any business being there! She promised me faithfully she'd go straight home. She has to start a picture tomorrow. She has to be on the set at seven-thirty. Let me talk to her!"

"I can't. She's dead."

"Now, Mr. Doan, I'm her manager, and I'm not going to argue…What did you say?"

"She's dead."

MacAdoo's voice went up a notch. "Now this is no time for jokes! She has to get her sleep, and she knows very well—"

"She's dead," Doan said patiently.

There was a long silence.

"Dead," said MacAdoo. "Oh, no. Oh, no, no!"

"At the Orna Apartments," Doan said. "On Harkness, just off Vine."

He put the telephone down and nodded at Arne.

Arne said, "She couldn't possibly have driven that far with that kind of a wound. I don't think she could have traveled a hundred yards. A wound of that type is fatal within minutes." He studied Doan for a second. "I'll notify the police. You two stay here and give them a statement. I don't want to appear as yet. There'll be no publicity of any kind—for twenty-four hours. I'll see to that."

He went out and shut the door behind him.

"I don't like him," Harriet said.

"He's getting on my nerves a bit, too," Doan answered absently.

Harriet looked down at Susan Sally. "I—I'll get a blanket and cover her up. It isn't nice for her to lie there . . ." She paused. "You know, I didn't like her, either, but I don't think anyone should have stabbed her like that."

"I don't think anyone should have, too," said Doan mildly.

Carstairs sat up and looked at him in a worried way.

Chapter14

EDMUND WASN'T ON DUTY THIS TIME WHEN Doan came down the stairs, and there was no one in the lobby except MacAdoo. He was sitting on a divan in the corner near the door, shoulders hunched, staring dully at the rug between his feet. He had his catalogue sombrero in his hands, and he was twisting the brim with a sort of dull thoroughness. His hair glistened in the light, oily and tightly curled and black, and his eyes were red-rimmed when he looked slowly up at Doan.

"Hello," he said hopelessly.

Doan nodded and sat down in the chair at the end of the divan.

"I came as fast as I could," MacAdoo said.

Doan nodded again.

"They wouldn't let me go upstairs," MacAdoo said. "They told me to stay down here and keep my mouth shut. They told me that Susan Sally's death wasn't to be released to the press. They said I had to stall the studio."

"Who said all this?"

"G-men," MacAdoo said. "FBI"

"They're hopping around this joint like fleas in a prison camp," Doan commented.

"I don't understand it," MacAdoo said. "I don't understand what Sally has to do with G-men. She has always paid her income tax right on the dot in full. I know, because I always have made it out for her."

Doan didn't say anything.

MacAdoo glanced at him. "Is she—is she—"

"She's gone. They took her away—to the morgue."

MacAdoo took out his handkerchief and blew his nose loudly. "I don't like that."

"Me, either," Doan said.

"It's not that I'm sentimental," MacAdoo declared. "No, sir. Between me and Sally, it was always strictly business and no nonsense...Oh, hell."

"Yeah," said Doan.

"I liked her."

"Me, too."

"She shouldn't ought to have been killed."

"That's right."

"She was too damned beautiful."

"You're on the beam," Doan agreed.

"A man would have to be cracked to kill anything as beautiful as that. Am I right?"

"Sure."

"That's going to make it tough to find out who did it, because Hollywood is practically packed with people who are cracked."

"That's no lie."

"You know who did it?"

"No. Not yet."

"I'd like to have a short interview with that party."

"After me," said Doan.

MacAdoo sighed. "Thirty-five hundred dollars a week. And no picture to picture contract, either. Forty straight weeks every year, whether she worked or not."

"How much did you get of that?" Doan asked.

MacAdoo sighed again, more deeply. "Ten per cent for being her agent, five per cent for being her business manager. That amounted to five hundred and twenty-five dollars a week. Oh, it was fair enough. I could have held her up for more. She was green as grass when I found her. And then, I had to spend all my time on her. I mean, she wasn't so easy to handle.

"She got notions. Like I had to save all my gas coupons so she could go to Heliotrope every once in awhile and give the rubes the ritz on account they used to shove her around when she was a kid. And then she was always associating with low characters. No offense."

Doan nodded. "Five and a quarter a week is a nice piece of change. Have you got any more clients like that lying around?"

"I haven't got any more clients, period. I'm flatter than a flounder at this point. I told you she took all my time. As an agent, I'm really not so hot, but you could hardly go wrong with something like Susan Sally, could you?"

"No."

"They come like that only once in a lifetime. I've had my quota."

"How'd you happen to get hold of her?"

MacAdoo began to untwist the brim of his hat. "I've always been interested in the theater. I thought I was an actor once, but nobody else did. I used to be a stagehand, and paint scenery and like that. Then I heard Hollywood was a soft touch, so I came out here. I never even got one job."

"Then what?"

"Well, I thought I'd better be an agent. That doesn't take any brains to speak of, and look at the dough they make. Look at the offices they sport on the Strip."

"Yeah."

"So I set up in business. It didn't work."

"No clients?" Doan asked.

"Anybody can get clients. I couldn't get the clients any jobs. Ten per cent of nothing won't keep you in beans for long."

"No," Doan agreed.

"So I was down to my carfare back to New York. I didn't even have anything to eat on going there. So I was down to the station, waiting for my train. And Susan Sally came up to me and asked me how to get to Hollywood, and the movie studios. She'd just come in on the train."

"What did you do?" Doan inquired.

"I took one look at her, and then went and cashed my ticket in. I got her to sign a contract in the taxi on the way back to Hollywood. I spent most of my ticket money renting an outfit for her, and I took her to the jazziest nightclub in town that night. Half an hour after we sat down in it there were three producers sitting with us, and three more trying to bribe the head waiter to throw out the first three. I mean, you couldn't miss with Susan Sally. I got her a contract that night, written on the front of a producer's dress shirt. It just happens once to one guy, Doan. It won't again for me. I'm all done now."

"Maybe not," said Doan.

MacAdoo nodded gloomily. "I know. Everybody in town has been drooling because I had her. Now they'll give me the brush-off, but quick. I'm back playing with peanuts again. You wouldn't want to let me handle that dog of yours, would you?"

"What?" said Doan.

"He's good. I saw some of the rushes of those defense films he made. Get him released from the government, and I could maybe make you a dime or two or three."

"I'll think it over. It would make him madder than hell though if he thought he was supporting me in luxury. He's old-fashioned. He thinks I ought to feed him instead of vice versa."

MacAdoo got up slowly and wearily. "I guess I'll go home again. It doesn't do me any good to sit here. Will you call me up if you hear anything new?"

"Sure."

"Good-by, Doan."

"Good-by," Doan said.

SALLY'S IN THE ALLEY97

MacAdoo went out the door, dragging his heels a little. Doan sat still, his face relaxed and bland and peaceful, until the switchboard buzzed softly. He got up, then, and went over to the desk and plugged in one of the outside lines.

"Yes?"

"Lemme speak to Doan."

"You are."

"I'm sure scared good and plenty now, Doanwashi. I sure am."

"That's too bad."

"You ain't gonna go back on your sworn word, are you?"

"Nope. Are you?"

"I guess not. Can you meet me at Hollywood and Cahuenga right away? In your car?"

"I'm on my way."

"Did you see the fella that shot at us?"

"No. Did you?"

"Man, I don't want to see him! Hurry up."

The line clicked, but it didn't hum. Doan waited for a moment, and then said:

"Well? "

Arne's voice said, "Go ahead and meet him. You still have about twenty-two hours."

"Keep out of my tracks," Doan warned. "I'm going to start huffing and puffing now."

Chapter 15

THE DIM-OUT HAS DONE A LOT FOR HOLLYWOOD Boulevard. It used to look just as cheap and cheesy as you'd think it would, and the types that clutter it up have been known to turn a strong man's stomach, but now it and they are shadowed discreetly, and it's not so bad. Of course, some very weird things come swimming out of the darkness now and then, but if you have steady nerves and a well balanced personality it is often possible to walk two or three blocks without having hysterics.

Doan rolled the Cadillac across on the signal and pulled in against the curb in the red zone on the far side and opened the door. Dust-Mouth popped out of the shadows and bounced on the front seat.

"Drive on!" he said breathlessly, slamming the door.

Doan pulled out into the traffic. "Somebody following you?"

"If they are, they sure must be dizzy by now. I been runnin' in circles for an hour."

"Where do you want to go?"

"Back to the desert. I wanta show you that there location. I wanta get this here deal all set. I don't like bein' shot at. That ain't good for a person."

"Not too much of it," Doan agreed.

Carstairs snorted twice imperiously from the back seat. Doan reached back and turned one of the windows down. Carstairs put his head outside.

"What's the matter with him?" Dust-Mouth demanded.

"He's a fresh air fiend." Doan said, turning the wing of his own window around so that the wind blew directly in his face. "So am I. You've got a new brand now, haven't you?"

"Of what?"

"Wine."

"Oh, yeah." Dust-Mouth took a round pint bottle out of his coat pocket. "This here is muscatel. It ain't as good as sherry, but it's better than nothin'. You want a drink?"

"No, thanks. Why don't you buy sherry?"

Dust-Mouth looked at him in surprise. "Winos drink sherry. They're nothin' but bums. If I was to go around buyin' it all the time, people would think I was one."

"Oh," said Doan.

"You got any dough on you, Doanwashi?"

"Some. Why?"

"Well, I was thinkin'. I'm still hot on that Ioway deal, but I got to have somethin' to live on until you Japs get there and take it over for me."

"I can spare you some eating money."

"Swell. Say, another thing."

"What?"

"How does the Jap government feel about puttin' people in insane asylums and such like?"

"They never do that. There's only one guy over there they keep a very close watch on."

"Who's he?"

"The Emperor."

"The head gazump, you mean? What's the matter with him?"

"He claims he's God."

"Wow!" said Dust-Mouth, awed. "I've met guys who thought they were Pontius Pilate and Judas and even the Pope, but I never hear of anybody who actually claimed he was God. This boy must be really nuts. Any chance of him recoverin'?"

"Yes," said Doan. "I think that someone will convince him he's wrong one day soon."

"That's good. He ain't runnin' the works in the meantime, is he?"

"No. They keep him under cover."

"I should think so. Even the Japs—no offense—ain't so dumb they'd believe a fandango like that."

"You'd be surprised," said Doan. "How'd you happen to run across this ore deposit?"

"Carbotetroberylthalium."

"What?" said Doan.

"That's it. I mean, that's pretty close to it, anyway. I looked it up again in the library. I can never remember that name."

"What's it good for?"

"I dunno. You put it in steel and it makes it harder or quicker or something. I guess."

"Maybe you'd better stop guessing," said Doan.

"Oh, it's the goods, all right. It's like this. I ran across it one time when I was goin' here and there. It had been washed out of a gully, and it was just layin' around there in the open. Just like them samples I showed you. So I picked up some of it just for hell and took it to this assayer I got credit with. I say, 'What the hell is this junk, Joe? I never see nothin' like it before.' So he foxes around and tests it and looks it up and all that, and then he tells me."

"What?"

"That it's what I tell you a minute ago. So I ask him what it's worth. And he says it ain't worth nothin', because they got mountains of the stuff stuck around here and there in foreign parts. So I forget it."

"What then?"

"So the dirty government cheats me, and we got a war. I still don't think nothin' about the junk until this assayer comes around and asks me about it again. He wants to know where I found it."

"Did you tell him?"

"Ha! Why, he's as big a crook as them guys in the government. Like as not he's hand in glove with 'em. Like as not he'd tell them where it was if I told him. So I let on like I'd forgot and got him to give me a grubstake to go find it again."

"You didn't, though."

"Hell, no. I got drunk. I knew where it was. I didn't have to hunt."

"What happened then?"

"The assayer got mad, but he give me another grubstake. So I got drunk again."

"And neat?"

"He got madder. So the stinker told the government on me, and they give me a grubstake. Only they sent a guy with me to see I hunted."

"What'd you do?"

"We both got drunk."

"Then what?"

"The crooks put me in an asylum. They figured to break down my character, but it didn't bother me a bit. I liked the place. Met a lot of interestin' folks. Had a good time."

"And after that?"

"As soon as the dirty government see I was enjoyin' myself they had me thrown out. They said they'd let me back in again if I showed 'em the deposit. But not me. I got principles."

"Sure," said Doan.

"So I went to Heliotrope. I told Peterkin I'd maybe tell him where the stuff was, so he was lettin' me stay in the jail. Nice jail, huh?"

"Yeah."

"Peterkin was watchin' me sort of, so I sent Tonto Charlie in to deal with this Pocus party."

"Did Tonto know where the deposit is?"

"Naw. I told him where it was, but I didn't tell him the right place. I figured he might not be honest. That's probably why Tonto got killed, I been thinkin'. He probably showed Pocus this place I told him, and there wasn't any ore there. Naturally that'd get Pocus upset."

"Naturally," Doan agreed.

"Oh, well," said Dust-Mouth, taking a drink. "Tonto Charlie ain't much of a loss, is he?"

"No, no," said Doan.

"I'm glad I'm dealin' with you instead of Pocus. He was a little too sudden to suit me. Although I hear you can sort of snort when you've got a mind to. They tell me you sort of run Parsley Jack into the ground."

"He slipped."

"Sure. He's in jail now."

"What for?"

"Evadin' the draft."

"How did that happen?"

"Oh, he was supposed to be inducted a long time ago. He was payin' Doc Gravelmeyer not to have him called. Doc is the head of the draft board in Heliotrope. When Parsley Jack run out when Doc was gonna give him a free operation, that made Doc almighty mad, so he had Parsley Jack pinched. He told Parsley Jack he'd let him go again if Jack would let Doc operate, but Jack said he preferred the Army."

"What's this Parsley Jack's relation to Free-Look Jones?"

"He just used to beat up people for Free-Look."

"For fun?"

"Mostly, I guess. Sometimes Free-Look would give him a beer or something if he beat up a guy real bad."

"I see," said Doan.

"Can you go any faster than this?"

"No. Why?"

"It's gonna rain. They even bust the radio silence on the weather to say so. Afraid of flash floods in the desert, I think, maybe. We got one flat to cross that might give us a bit of trouble."

"We'll worry about that when we come to it."

Chapter 16

THE CADILLAC CRAWLED ALONG LIKE A BUG under a bucket, and the simile is all the more apt because this was no ordinary desert day. They are merely unpleasant. This one had a tinge of horror tucked around its edges. The sky was a gunmetal gray with dark, jagged streaks groping through it like a witch's fingers.

The wind was a solid, chill mass of pressure that blew without stopping, and the mesquite bush cringed under it, and even the cactus leaned queasily away. It was strong enough so that Doan had to exert constant force on the steering wheel to keep the car from hopping out of the scarred, straggling ruts to march off into the brush on a tour of its own.

"You sure you know where you are?" he asked.

"Yeah, man," said Dust-Mouth. "Just keep plugging along. Not so far now."

The road wandered up the side of a hill, switching back and forth. The springs hit bottom with a bang, and Carstairs mumbled critically in Doan's ear.

"Shutup," said Doan. "I didn't build this road, and you can be damned sure I didn't invent this desert."

He shifted into second gear. The Cadillac heaved up over the top of the hill, and the desert stretched away in front of them, barren and twisted and empty, with rocks, much too reminiscent of tombstones, pushing up through the sand at odd intervals.

The wind paused just long enough to draw a breath, and then hit them with a bushel of blown sand that scraped like fingernails on a slate.

Doan winced. "This isn't doing my paint any good."

"Nope," Dust-Mouth agreed cheerfully. "Sand will take it off neat as pie. Probably scar up all your windows so you can't see through 'em, too."

The car crawled down into a valley and twisted back around, through rocks that were cold and black and malevolently twisted. Lights flickered quickly along the horizon, and after a while the thunder bumbled sullenly to itself.

"What happens to the road when it rains?" Doan inquired.

"What road?"

"This one!"

"Oh. This ain't really a road. It's a sort of a path, you might say. When it gets washed out, you just make a new one."

"Fine stuff," Doan commented. "When is it going to rain, or was that just a rumor?"

"Storm's over behind the Crazy Legs now. When she comes around that mountain yonder she won't be drivin' six white horses, but she'll sure be comin'. Keep goin'."

The Cadillac topped another hill, and without any warning lightning flicked at them like a gigantic whip in a green, crackling glare that raised the hair on Doan's head. The thunder hit instantly, not in a roll, but in a blasting report that lifted the Cadillac and slammed it down again.

"Wow!" said Doan groggily.

"Hit back of us in the valley," Dust-Mouth reported. "Reckon there must be some iron in them rocks."

Lightning flicked again, and thunder slammed them back in their seats, and a green spitting ball of fire as big as a house went hopping with terrible daintiness down the slope ahead of them and struck a rock head on and split it neatly in two. The thin, cringing stink of brimstone floated in the wind.

"Did you—see what I saw?" Doan asked.

"Yeah, man," said Dust-Mouth soberly.

A solid gray curtain appeared ahead of them. It marched remorselessly forward over hill and dale, and hit them solidly. It resembled rain just about as much as Niagara Falls does. The Cadillac crouched down under the weight of it, and Doan could see all of a good ten feet ahead of his radiator ornament.

Dust-Mouth pounded him on the shoulder. "Go on! Drown us here!"

Doan turned on the windshield wipers, and effortlessly the wind twisted them loose and threw them aside. It blew out a section of rubber padding around the side window, and rain drops whipped in and hit him in the face like individual needles.

Dust-Mouth pounded his shoulder again. "Stop! Wait!"

Doan halted the car. It rocked ominously. Dust-Mouth was fighting with the door handle on his side.

"What are you doing?" Doan shouted.

"Out. Test road."

Dust-Mouth got the door open and fell out. The wind snatched the door out of his grasp and slammed it hard enough to rock the car even more violently. It spun Dust-Mouth around and knocked him against the front fender. The rain hit him, but it didn't soak in. It bounced.

He fought for his balance, finally got it. Bent over nearly double, he staggered ahead. He was a grotesque shadow stamping and dancing on the road edge. His arms flung and beckoned wildly.

Doan drove ahead in low. The Cadillac slewed gently. Doan fed it more gas, and it caught itself with a jerk and ground on around the edge of a knoll.

Dust-Mouth hauled the door open and fell inside. He was panting brokenly.

"Two hundred foot drop," he said. "On your side. Road edge crumbled under your rear wheel. You feel it?"

"Yes," said Doan.

"Go down now. Faster. Let her roll."

The car heaved and banged down the slope, lurching with a sort of giddy dignity. The road leveled out and straightened, water glimmering cold and metallic in the ruts.

"Faster!" Dust-Mouth yelled. "Faster!"

Doan fed it the gas, and the car rolled stubbornlyforward. Brush crackled damply under the fenders. "Faster!" Dust-Mouth yelled. "Oh, God! We'll never make it!"

Water sucked and gurgled evilly under them, brown streaked with rust-red, surface whipped into a froth of scummed bubbles. It tore at the front wheels and lapped eagerly at the fenders and seeped in coldly along the floor boards. Carstairs yelped indignantly and jumped up on the rear seat, arching his back like a cat.

Doan could feel the sand sliding away under the tires.

"Oh, God," said Dust-Mouth numbly.

The Cadillac twitched its rear end like an irritated dowager, and began to climb straight up a cut-bank. It skidded on the top, dipped daintily, made it with a defiant roar. The wheels spun and stopped.

"Well?" said Doan, wiping the perspiration and rain moisture off his face.

"Whew," said Dust-Mouth. "That there was the flat I spoke to you about."

"What was in it?"

"A flash flood. It'll maybe rise ten feet in five minutes. We're safe here, though."

"What'll we do—camp?"

"Naw. There's a shack just beyond that hump. I think we better hole up. I don't think we better drive no further right now."

"I don't think so, either."

They got out of the car and stood against the drive of the rain. The wind rippled the fur on Carstairs' back, and he ducked his head between his shoulders, glaring at Doan in squint-eyed disgust.

"Where the hell are we from that deposit?" Doan shouted, shielding his eyes with a raised forearm.

"Here."

"What?"

"It's right here. We're standing on it. All through this flat here. That's how I spotted it. Another flood washed some out in the flat."

"Where's the shack, then? Let's go."

"Come on—"

Edmund stepped out from behind the car. He had his coat collar turned up, and his left hand grasped it tight around his throat. His hair was plastered flat and slick down over his forehead, and water ran down from it in jagged streaks. He was holding a stubby, shiny revolver in his right hand.

"Well, Edmund, my boy," said Doan. "How are you and all that?"

Edmund's lips looked white and stiff. "Put your hands up."

"Sure," said Doan amiably, raising them.

"Keep your dog close."

"Come here, stupid," Doan ordered.

Carstairs edged in reluctantly against his leg.

"I surprised you," said Edmund.

"Well, yes," Doan admitted. "You might say you did, to some extent. How'd you get here?"

"I came with you—in your luggage compartment."

"Well, well," said Doan.

Edmund lifted his upper lip. "You didn't think, did you, Mr. Doan, that during the course of your nonsensical and childish game of pretending to be an enemy agent that you might run across a real one?"

"I wouldn't want to upset you or disappoint you at this moment," Doan answered, "but yes. I had an idea I might. I must admit that I didn't think it would be you, though. It's too bad, too. I mean, you were a pretty good desk clerk. As a spy, I can't give you so much."

"What?" Dust-Mouth exclaimed suddenly. "Hey!"

Edmund's shiny revolver moved an inch. "I told you to put up your hands."

"Who are you?" Dust-Mouth bellowed.

"Meet my pal, Edmund," Doan said. "He was the desk clerk at the Orna Apartment Hotel in the good old days."

"He said he was a spy!"

"I heard that, too."

"What's he doin' here?"

"Pointing a gun at you. Haven't you noticed?"

"You'd better put up your hands," said Edmund.

"Why, you little stinker," said Dust-Mouth. "Gimme that gun before I make you eat it."

He took a step forward, lowering his head.

"Look out!" Doan yelled.

Edmund fired. The wind took the sound of the report and shredded it and whipped the remnants away. Dust-Mouth turned around and stumbled on legs that were suddenly loose and wobbly under him, and then he went down headlong, and the rain splashed and stained itself on his face.

Edmund's tongue flicked across his lips. Doan stood rigid. Edmund breathed in slowly at last, and Doan relaxed just slightly.

"That is what happens to people who don't do what I tell them," Edmund said.

"Sure," said Doan.

"Roll him over the bank. Keep your hands up."

Doan inserted his toe under Dust-Mouth's body and flopped him over, once and then again. The edge of the cut-bank crumbled, and Dust-Mouth went down the steep side of it like a ragged, molting bundle. The roiled water splashed coldly over him. It heaved his body up once, and he stared at Doan with eyes that were wide and amazed under the red hole in his forehead, and then the water flipped him over much as Doan had done and dragged him greedily down out of sight.

"All right," said Doan. "What's next?"

Edmund felt behind him and opened the rear door of the Cadillac. "Tell your dog to get in there," he said, sidling away from the car.

"Get in," Doan said, nudging Carstairs with his knee.

Carstairs climbed slowly into the car. Edmund slammed the door. "Turn around."

Doan turned around. Edmund came closer and pushed the shiny revolver against his spine.

"Don't move."

Doan stood still. Edmund's hand slid lightly over his shoulder and retrieved the .25 automatic from the breast pocket of his coat. The hand disappeared, came back empty, and slipped the Police Positive out of Doan's waistband.

Edmund moved backward cautiously. "Open the door and let the dog out. Keep him close to you."

Doan obeyed. Carstairs sat down on the sand, his ears tucked low against the whip of the wind, and examined Edmund with a sort of speculative interest.

"Well?" said Doan, doing the same.

"We'll go to the shack," said Edmund. "There are some things I wish you to tell me. Walk that way. Walk slowly. Keep your hand on the dog's collar. I'll shoot you instantly if you don't do exactly as I say."

Doan turned around and headed into the wind with Carstairs walking beside him. The rain slashed at Doan's face in slanting flicks, and the sand packed heavily on his shoes. The faint straggle of a path led around a knoll and through scarred, knee high brush, and then the shack loomed at a little higher level across the draw in front of them.

It was small, no more than about twelve-by-twelve, made of odd-size lumber that had weathered and warped, and it had a roof shingled with flattened five-gallon tins and a stovepipe chimney that drooped disconsolately.

Doan stopped when he saw it.

"Go on," Edmund ordered.

"You've got visitors."

"What?"

"There's someone inside," Doan said. "If they're friends of yours, it's okay by me, but I wouldn't like to get caught in a crossfire."

The revolver nudged into Doan's spine again, and he could sense rather than hear Edmund's heavy breathing just back of his ear.

"How do you know there's someone inside?"

Doan pointed down. Carstairs was staring at the but with his ears pricked forward sharply, his head tilted a little. The stunted brush along the sides of the draw clashed and chittered uneasily, and rain ran curiously around among exposed roots.

Edmund moved closer against Doan's back. "Hello!" he shouted suddenly. "Hello!"

A voice came back like a flat, muffled echo. "Hello!"

Edmund sighed noisily. "It's all right. Go ahead."

Doan dug his heels in and slid down the bank. The sand at the bottom of the draw sucked mushily under his shoes, and he climbed up the other side, skidding slightly.

The braced door of the shack moved a little, uncertainly, and then opened back and revealed a square of dim, blue gloom. Rain slapped and spattered on the tin roofing and drooled messily down from the eaves.

"Inside," said Edmund.

Doan and Carstairs edged through the door.

"Why, Mr. Doan," said Harriet Hathaway.

She was sitting down on the floor against the wall at Doan's right with her feet out in front of her. Blue was sitting beside her with his feet out, too. He was studying them with gloomily absorbed interest. He looked like a man who has been suspecting the worst and has just found out that it is all too true.

MacAdoo was sitting on a nail keg against the opposite wall. His sombrero was spotted blackly with rain, and some of the colors had run from the band across its wide, tilted brim. He looked worried, but not about the rifle he was holding on his lap. He seemed to be quite at home with that.

"Don't tell me," said Doan. "Let me guess. It's old home week."

Edmund shoved the revolver against his back. "Get out of the way."

Doan and Carstairs stepped sideways in concert.

"Hello," MacAdoo said to Edmund.

"So it's you," said Edmund. "What do you mean by coming here?"

MacAdoo moved the rifle to indicate Harriet and Blue. "They were following you. I followed them. I thought I'd best collect them and bring them along."

"What were you following me for?" Edmund asked.

"Oh, you," said Harriet. "What would anyone want to follow you for? I mean, you're just a desk clerk. I mean, we weren't following you at all. We didn't even see you. We were following Mr. Doan."

"Why?" Doan asked.

"You were acting suspiciously. Sneaking."

"Don't blame me," said Blue. "I was agin the whole idea." He had shaved, and his skin looked new and pink and polished. He still wore his black glasses.

"Well, you know it was a good idea," Harriet told him. "Just look.

I mean, it's obvious that there is some kind of a subversive plot going on somewhere. Just why are you neglecting your duties in this frivolous manner, Mr. Doan?"

"Ask Edmund," Doan advised.

"Be quiet," said Edmund. "Speak when you're spoken to." He nodded coldly at MacAdoo. "How did you get here ahead of us?"

"Drove," MacAdoo answered. "I've got no governor on my car. I passed you back at the crossroads."

"Well, why did you come here?"

"I thought—"

"Tchah!" said Edmund contemptuously. "Thought! You do nothing but think. This is a time for action, not thinking. You should have killed them somewhere else."

"What?" said Harriet.

"Who?" said Blue.

"Tchah!" Edmund said. "When you meddle, you die."

"It's no act," Doan told them. "He means it."

"But why?" Harriet demanded shakily.

"Be quiet," Edmund ordered. "Perhaps I will rape you before I kill you, although I don't think it would be worth my time. You." He jabbed the revolver at Doan. "Sit down there beside them. Keep your hands folded in your lap."

Doan sat down and extended his feet. Carstairs sat down in front of him.

"Where'd you get that rifle?" Edmund asked MacAdoo.

"Bought it."

"What kind is it?"

"Mannlicher 6.5 sporter with a five power scope."

"Tchah!" said Edmund. "Austrian. You."

"Present," Doan answered.

"Where is the ore deposit?"

"We're sitting on it."

"No," said Edmund. "The other one, Tonto Charlie, brought me here. There is no ore in this area that could be of any possible use to any government. Right?"

MacAdoo nodded. "Right."

"I'm blanked, then," Doan said. "Why don't you ask Blue?"

"Huh?" said Blue.

"Don't be silly," Harriet said sharply. "Blue doesn't know anything about ore. He doesn't know anything about anything. Do you?"

"Nope," said Blue.

"Hmmm," said Edmund, watching him. "You are too stupid to be real. You are not even a good actor. What do you know about this matter?"

"Nothin'."

"You'd better answer," Edmund said. "I'm very impatient."

Doan was staring narrowly at the back of Carstairs' neck. Carstairs flicked his ears twice and then finally turned around to stare at him. Doan stopped looking at his neck and began studying the door. It was not latched. The wind moved it slightly, and the bottom edge scraped on the rough floor.

Carstairs began to watch the door, too.

Harriet said, "You're a very silly person. I think you're getting a little above yourself, aren't you? Going around kidnaping people and threatening them. There are laws—"

"If you don't keep quiet I'll kick you in the face," Edmund told her.

Blue sighed drearily. "I dunno why I had to get mixed up with such people."

The wind moved the door back a little more. The muscles along Carstairs' back quivered slightly.

"Edmund," Doan said.

Edmund turned toward him. "What?"

"Which brand of enemy agent are you?"

Edmund's lip curled. "Need you ask?"

"Not any more," said Doan. "What were you doing as a desk clerk?"

"Preparing to get in an aircraft factory."

"I see," said Doan. "That would be—*Hike!*"

Carstairs moved in a blurred streak. He hit the edge of the door with one shoulder and knocked it wider open and slipped through.

Edmund whirled around and fired. Carstairs was in midair, taking off from the threshold. He turned clear over in the air with a breathless grunt, slammed down on his side, and skidded out of sight down into the draw.

"You!" said Edmund to Doan, white-faced. He whirled again and snatched the rifle out of MacAdoo's hands. "I hit him! He won't go far!

I'll follow . . . Take this! Watch! Make no mistakes!" He thrust the shiny revolver at MacAdoo and ran headlong out the door.

MacAdoo settled the revolver competently in his palm. He still looked worried, but no more so than he had before.

"No more tricks," he warned. "I'm not quite as bloodthirsty as Edmund, but I have some few instincts of self defense."

He got up off the nail keg, holding the revolver carefully leveled, and shut the door tight. He walked backward to the nail keg and sat down again. The rain thrummed noisily on the roof.

"I don't think I like Edmund," Doan said conversationally.

"No one does," said MacAdoo. "Naturally. He's a graduate of the *Ordensburgen.*"

"What are that?"

"Where they train the *Geheim Staatspolizei.* The Gestapo. Their graduates are very clever. They are given a very thorough education in how to assume any particular background they might choose. Edmund's slang and mannerisms are good, I think."

"Very good," Doan agreed. "Do you go around heiling Hitler, too?"

"Adolf? No. Although I've always rather liked him."

"You talk as though you knew him."

"I do."

"I mean, personally."

MacAdoo nodded. "Yes. I do."

Harriet gasped. "You know Adolf Hitler?"

"Certainly," said MacAdoo.

"That's horrible!"

"No, it isn't. He's rather amusing sometimes. Better than the radio. That is, he was. I understand he's run to seed a bit lately"

"How'd you happen to meet him?" Doan asked.

"I ran an art shop in Munich for several years. He used to hang around and cadge coffee money off me. I sold a couple of his pictures."

"They're terrible pictures!" Harriet snapped. "Everybody knows they're just old house-painter's smears."

"No, they're not," said MacAdoo. "They're not bad at all. They're not wonderful, but they're pretty competent jobs of work. I wonder why you Americans always have to try to make anything your enemies do seem ridiculous and bungling. It causes you a lot of needless casualties."

"You ain't lyin'," Blue said.

"Why what do you know about it?" Harriet demanded.

"He was maybe thinking of airplanes," Doan suggested.

Harriet stared at him. "Everyone knows that our planes are the best in the world and that the German planes are nothing but a lot of old junk and ersatz, and that their pilots are all cowards."

"Sure," said Doan. "MacAdoo, if you were kicking around in Munich when Hitler was trying to sell pictures, how come you didn't hitch up with the Nazis when they started going?"

"I did. I've got party card number eleven."

"What does that mean?" Harriet inquired coldly.

"It means there were a total of ten Nazis, including Hitler, when I joined up. I didn't join, really. Hitler presented me with a membership when I asked him to pay me back some of the dough I'd lent him."

"That must have sort of put you in on the ground floor," Doan said thoughtfully.

"Yes."

"You ought to have cleaned up when the Nazis began to get rolling."

"I did."

"How?" Doan asked.

"I was art director of the *Reich.* I—ah—bought pictures from people and—ah—sold them to other people."

Doan said, "You mean you confiscated pictures from Hitler's enemies, and blackmailed people who wanted to be his friends into buying them."

"That's putting it very crudely," said MacAdoo, "but lucidly."

"Did you have a monopoly on that business?"

"Yes."

"You must have put away plenty."

"I did."

"What'd you stop for?"

MacAdoo's lips tightened. "Goering. That big tub of guts. He was building castles all over Germany, and he informed me I should donate pictures for them. He had a list of the pictures. The most valuable ones I had—ah—purchased. Imagine that. I should give him pictures. He wasn't satisfied with stealing all the steel mills in Germany, he's got to cut in on my business."

"What did you do?" Doan inquired.

"Told him to go to hell."

"What did he do?"

"Tried to murder me six times within six days. I had a few body-guards of my own, of course, but even then he had ten regiments of thugs plus the air force. I had to cut and run for it. I'm going to get even with him for that one of these fine days. I'll probably have to wait until after the war, I suppose."

"Goering is going to be hung after we win the war," Harriet told him.

MacAdoo looked at her. "Don't be silly. The Kaiser didn't have much more than a hundred million dollars, and nobody hung him. Goering is worth two or three billion by this time, and besides that he has heavy influence in England and the United States."

"How do you know?" Doan asked.

"Read the papers. Who do you think is paying for all this bilge about Goering being a harmless, jolly fat man with a love for medals and a heart of gold? Stuff like that isn't printed for free. Particularly not after the guy involved has murdered a half million civilians with his air force. I shouldn't wonder but what he'll wind up as president of the *Reich* under a, pause for laughter, democratic government."

MacAdoo leaned sideways on his nail keg and pulled a leather covered flask from his hip pocket. He snapped the patented top open with his teeth.

"Have some brandy?"

"No, thanks," said Doan. "Edmund's taking a long time, isn't he?"

MacAdoo smiled. "Isn't he? He'll be back, though. Are you think-ing about the FBI? Don't. They won't be around. They didn't follow you. I believe they had an idea of scouting for you in a plane, but one couldn't get off the ground in this kind of weather, and if it did no one in it would be able to see anything."

"Hmmm," said Doan. "How'd you get into the country, and stay so long without being spotted? They must have a record and pictures of you."

"There are ways. They do have pictures of me, but in the pictures I was forty pounds heavier, bald, wore a beard, and had a hooked nose."

"Oh. What'll you look like tomorrow?"

"Not like I did then or do now."

"How'd Edmund spot you?"

"Goering. He's never quit trying to find me. He finally did."

"How come he didn't try some more murder?"

"I got in touch with Adolf. I told him to call Goering off, or I'd start talking to the United States Government, and not about pictures, either."

"Edmund doesn't like you very well."

"No. He thinks I'm a party backslider."

"When are you going to kill him?" Doan asked.

"After he attends to you"

The thin, distant crack of a rifle sounded somewhere outside. It was repeated almost instantly.

"That's the end of your dog," said MacAdoo. "He never had a chance. Edmund is an expert killer."

"Too bad," said Doan. "But then, I never liked Carstairs much anyway. Do you think he really could have gotten a job in pictures?"

"I think so."

"How about me?"

"No," said MacAdoo.

Doan sighed. "That's what comes of having brains instead of beauty."

The rain rippled musically on the roof, and the wind brushed tentative, prying fingers along the wall of the shack.

"I don't understand this!" Harriet wailed suddenly.

Doan sighed again. "I might as well tell all, I guess. We might have a long—wait."

MacAdoo chuckled. "Edmund will come back."

Doan said, "The FBI delegated me to find out the location of an ore deposit from a man named Dust-Mouth Haggerty."

"Then why didn't you do it?" Harriet demanded.

"There wasn't any such deposit."

"How long have you known that?" MacAdoo asked.

"Oh, for some time. I'm not as dumb as Edmund."

MacAdoo nodded. "He is very stupid. I don't know what they must be thinking of in Germany. Even Americans aren't complete fools—not all of them."

"Tell me more!" Harriet commanded.

Doan said, "Dust-Mouth claimed to know where some strategically valuable ore was. He didn't. There wasn't any. The FBI were pretty sure of that, but not completely. They used Dust-Mouth and me for bait, and they pulled in quite a haul."

"You shouldn't have taken the job," said MacAdoo.

"Don't I know it? I didn't want to. Every time I work for the government, I get put in jail. I'll bet if I got out of this, they'd slap me away for something."

"You don't have to worry—about jail," said MacAdoo.

"I wonder where Edmund is?"

"He'll come. He's probably burying your dog."

"Well, why did Dust-Mouth say he knew where some ore was if he didn't?" Harriet said angrily.

"He made a business out of it. He got free room and board because people thought they could make a million out of him. He was a very dumb guy. He was playing with fire all the time and didn't have sense enough to know it. He had taken plenty of suckers on phony claims in his day, and he didn't realize that in wartime the suckers might not just laugh it off. He didn't even know what kind of ore he was supposed to have. He had a collection of samples, and he just agreed they contained whatever you said. If you didn't say, he made something up."

"Past tense?" MacAdoo inquired.

Doan nodded. "Edmund."

"Oh," said MacAdoo.

"The FBI thought he might be playing a little deeper game than he was. So did I."

"What were you going to do with him out here?" MacAdoo asked.

"Toast his tootsies over a match flame until he told me who killed Tonto Charlie and Free-Look Jones and Susan Sally."

"Well, who did?" Harriet asked.

"Edmund," said Doan. "Just old Edmund. The fellow we're waiting for. I wonder if he's reading a burial service over Carstairs? Dust-Mouth heard in Heliotrope that I was a Jap agent. The FBI did that. They even furnished my address. Dust-Mouth was getting short of customers, so he figured he might take a little dough off of me. He sent Tonto Charlie to see me. Tonto ran into Edmund. Edmund bit. That was bad luck for Tonto, because Edmund doesn't have much of a sense of humor. Tonto brought him out here and showed him what was supposed to be some kind of valuable ore." Doan looked at MacAdoo. "Is that when Edmund got in touch with you?"

MacAdoo nodded. "Yes. He wanted samples assayed. I had it done for him. The samples showed no traces of any ore worth a dime to anybody for anything."

"Bing," said Doan. "Good-by, Tonto Charlie. He was hiding out at the Orna in Edmund's apartment at the time, waiting for the assayer's report. Tonto actually thought Dust-Mouth did have something. Edmund got mad and stabbed him, and then he had a body."

"As I said, he is very stupid," MacAdoo agreed.

"Comes the FBI looking for Doan," said Doan. "Edmund gets a little nervous about his body. I mean, Tonto's. The FBI park a car in front of the door where Edmund can see it and go away. Edmund finds gas ration books made out in my name in the car. A light dawns. He sends the garage attendant or janitor or whoever away on an errand, drives the car into the basement garage, gets Tonto Charlie's body and sticks it in the luggage compartment, and drives the car back to the front of the apartment and parks it. Now Doan has a body."

"Oh!" said Harriet.

"I thought it belonged to you," Doan told her. "I thought your pal, here, stuck it in the car when I stopped for you in the desert. That's why I wanted to keep you sort of under my eye for the time being."

"Oh!" said Harriet.

"I'm cold," said Blue. "Sure wish I was back on my reservation."

"Don't these horrible things you've been hearing make you want to join the Army and fight, fight, fight?" Harriet demanded.

"No," said Blue glumly.

"You're a coward!"

"I sure am," said Blue. "I guess you hate me now, huh?"

"Well . . ." said Harriet. "No. I—I don't."

"Oh," said Blue, sighing.

"And then there was Free-Look Jones," said Doan. "He was the sort of gent who would lay his hand to anything. He had been sniffing around behind Dust-Mouth and his make-believe ore. Edmund snared him, too, and signed him up. That's why he jumped me. He wanted me to get into a riot and get my car searched. He missed, and when Tonto Charlie mysteriously turned up with Free-Look's knife in his throat, he got too hot. Edmund put him away. How did Edmund get to Heliotrope?"

"With Susan Sally and me," MacAdoo said.

"I thought so. That's what she wanted to tell me, wasn't it?"

"Yes. Edmund talked too much in front of her. I may have done a little of that myself, at one time or another."

"Edmund killed her. Very neatly, too. She didn't know he had done it until she was dead"

"Very neatly," MacAdoo agreed. "They teach you those things at the *Ordensburgen.*"

"He took her up in the elevator," Doan said. "He tripped her when she got out, didn't he?"

"Yes," said MacAdoo.

"And when she fell he fell on top of her, hard."

"Yes," said MacAdoo.

"He knocked the breath out of her and stabbed her in that instant. He knew just how and where. Then he picked her up and brushed her off and apologized. She was dying right then, but she didn't know it. It takes a little while, with that kind of a stab wound, for the pain to catch up with you."

"Yes," MacAdoo said woodenly.

"She thought she was just breathless and bruised a bit. Edmund steered her toward my apartment and then ran downstairs and started figuring on his radio diagram. That was very clever. He was so obviously right on the spot that he figured I wouldn't believe it. Aside from that, he's a swell actor, and he's just stupid enough to take all kinds of screwy risks without counting up the odds against him. He knew what I was going to do before I did it most of the time. He listened in on all my telephone conversations and spied on me in every other way he could find. He was in the luggage compartment again when I went to see Dust-Mouth first last night. At that time he still thought Dust-Mouth might have something. He prevented Dust-Mouth from telling me what it was. And then he tried to point the finger at you."

"Me?" said Blue.

"Yeah. He knew you were a phony, but not what kind of a one."

"Do you know?" said Blue.

"Sure. Since you shaved."

"What?" Harriet snapped.

"Haven't you spotted him yet? Blue is just his nickname. His real name is Roger Laws. Blue Laws, they call him."

"Whu-whu-whu-what ?"

"How are the eyes now?" Doan asked Blue.

"Okay. I'll be able to ditch these glasses soon."

Harriet screamed.

Blue glanced at her with distaste. "What now?"

"You're the ace! The fighter pilot! Tuh-twenty-five enemy planes!"

"Twenty-seven," Doan corrected.

"You're a huh-hero!" Harriet wailed. "You were sh-shot down in flames!"

"Three times," Blue agreed sourly. "And don't talk to me about German planes and pilots. I don't fall five miles for fun. Anybody that knocks me down has to be better than I am, and I'm damned good."

"Oh—my—yes!"

"Shutup."

"Oh! You're won-wonderful !"

"Oh, nuts," said Blue.

"Why the dumbbell act?" Doan inquired.

Blue jerked his thumb at Harriet. "After this performance, you can ask?"

Harriet reached out her hand and touched his sleeve reverently with her fingertips.

"Get away," said Blue.

Harriet stared at him, shiny-eyed.

"Oh, my God!" Blue snarled. "Will you stop that? Listen. I like to fly. I like to shoot planes down. It's very interesting work. It pays well. I even get a pension when I retire."

"You mean—if," said Doan.

"Ooooh," said Harriet.

"Get away from me! Damn you, I acted as dumb as I could to get rid of you, but no matter how I tried I couldn't act one tenth as dumb as you can without trying!"

"Yes, Blue," said Harriet, entranced.

"You've got no more brains than a rabbit."

"No, Blue."

"You make me sick."

"Yes, Blue. I love you."

"Oh, shutup."

"Now I can die happily—with you."

"Dying is no fun," Blue said. "I've already tried it a couple times."

MacAdoo was looking more worried now. "I wish I'd known. I wish I had."

"What eats him?" Blue asked Doan.

"Goering," said Doan.

"Come again."

"You shoot down Goering's men. MacAdoo loves you like a brother for that."

MacAdoo nodded. "I only wish I'd known. I'd have thought of something else. Now it's too late."

"Maybe not," said Doan.

MacAdoo said, "I'll shoot if you move your hands again."

"Edmund, dear Edmund," said Doan, "please come home to me now."

"Where is Edmund?" Blue inquired slowly.

"Ah," said Doan knowingly.

Watching Doan, MacAdoo took a drink out of his flask and put it down again carefully on the floor beside him.

"Of course," Doan said judicially, "MacAdoo wouldn't have to wait for Edmund. He could just shoot us."

"Could he?" said Blue.

There was a little film of sweat on McAdoo's forehead. "Sit still," he said.

"I'm not moving a muscle," said Doan. "Neither is Blue. Are you?"

"Nope," said Blue. "I wonder if Edmund got lost."

"Sure," said Doan. "That's it. He's wandering around in the desert, with nothing to drink but a flash flood."

"Too bad," said Blue, "but then MacAdoo was going to kill him anyway. Why?"

"He killed Susan Sally," said Doan. "He shouldn't have done that. She was worth five and a quarter a week to MacAdoo."

"Shutup," said MacAdoo thinly.

"Why, sure," said Doan.

The rain clattered nerve-rackingly on the tin above them and gurgled and choked under the eaves.

MacAdoo sighed a little and got up from the nail keg. He began to move toward the door, side-stepping carefully. He reached it and felt for the latch with his left hand, keeping the revolver leveled in his right.

The latch clicked, and MacAdoo pulled the door open and turned his head quickly. He didn't have time to do anything else voluntarily. Carstairs must have been about ten feet away, waiting, and he had started to run as soon as the door moved. His chest hit MacAdoo shoulder high with the force of a battering ram, and his jaws snapped across MacAdoo's face with an ugly, sliding squeak of teeth on bone.

MacAdoo went clear the length of the shack and hit the back wall hard enough to bulge it. He slammed down full length on the floor with both hands clapped over his face and the blood running red and thick through his fingers. He began to shriek in a high, bubbling voice, writhing around in blind circles on the floor, arching his body up in the middle.

Doan was on his feet instantly. He caught Carstairs by the collar and hauled, exerting all his strength.

"Back! Back!"

Carstairs allowed himself to go back one reluctant step.

Doan nodded to Blue and then pointed at MacAdoo. "Hold him down."

Blue got up and then knelt with one knee on MacAdoo's chest. MacAdoo kept right on shrieking. Doan measured carefully and then kicked. His toe caught MacAdoo in the temple. MacAdoo's head jarred sideways, and then his body loosened and went limp. He stopped shrieking.

"He was right," Doan said thoughtfully. "Come to think of it, I don't believe he will look the same tomorrow."

"Oh, oh, oh, oh," Harriet moaned.

"Shut up," said Blue. "Did you want him yelling like that all the way back to town?"

Harriet made little gulping sounds.

Blue sat down beside her and put his arm around her shoulders. He pulled her head against his chest.

"Okay. It wasn't nice to see. Don't look any more."

"I was scu-scared."

"Hell, so was I."

"I love you."

"Sure," said Blue.

There was a silence.

"Go ahead and say it," Doan ordered. "She deserves it."

"I love you, too," said Blue reluctantly.

"Oh, Blue. Oh."

"Let's take a look at you," Doan said to Carstairs. "Oh-oh. Too dumb to duck, huh?"

There was a deep red groove through the muscles of Carstairs' shoulder, and blood had run down from it and formed in ugly clots on his chest and leg.

"What happened to Edmund?" Blue asked.

"They probably taught him about tracking in the spy school," Doan said absently. "But I guess they forgot to tell him that when you're tracking something like Carstairs, you should watch behind as well as in front. Carstairs just circled and jumped on his back when he went by. I'm afraid dear old Edmund is deader than a doornail."

"How can you be sure of that?"

"It makes Carstairs mad to be shot. Offhand I can't think of anyone who ever did it that lived to talk about it, and Edmund wouldn't be the exception. Hold still."

Doan picked up MacAdoo's flask and straddled Carstairs, one leg on either side of him.

"This'll hurt, maybe."

He poured from the flask carefully. Carstairs grunted and arched his back violently. Doan sat down hard on the floor, carefully holding the flask right side up.

"Okay," he said. He sniffed once and then grinned. "Ahem. Have you been drinking, my friend?"

Very slowly Carstairs turned his head toward his shoulder and sniffed. Just as slowly he turned his head back to look at Doan.

"Aw, now," said Doan. "I was only clowning."

Carstairs turned around and started for the door. Doan scrooched along hurriedly, bump-bottom fashion, and grabbed him by the tail.

"Wait! Can't you take a joke?"

Carstairs sat down with his back to him.

Doan scrooched around in front of him. "Now, look. I had to put something on that groove, or it'd have gotten infected. Would you like to go to a dog hospital and associate with a lot of curs with only ordinary pedigrees?"

Carstairs turned his head aside.

"Look, Carstairs," Doan said. "Look."

He tilted the flask and swallowed in big gulps. He choked and then held the flask over his head and sprinkled liquor over himself like a shower.

"See? Now if you just stay close to me everyone will think I'm drunk and they're smelling me. Get it? I'm drunk. Whoopee. Whee."

Carstairs looked at him for a long time in a thoughtful, dispassionate way. Doan beamed back. Carstairs fetched a sigh from the bottom of his heart and then lay down and closed his eyes in soul-weary resignation.

THE END

About The Rue Morgue Press

The Rue Morgue vintage mystery line is designed to bring back into print those books that were favorites of readers between the turn of the century and the 1960s. The editors welcome suggests for reprints. To receive our catalog or make suggestions, write The Rue Morgue Press, P.O. Box 4119, Boulder, Colorado (1-800-669-6214). The Rue Morgue Press tries to keep all of its titles in print, though some books may go temporarily out of print for up to six months. The following list details the titles available as of September 2001.

Catalog of Rue Morgue Press titles January 2002

Titles are listed by author. All books are quality trade paperbacks measuring 9 by 6 inches, usually with full-color covers and printed on paper designed not to yellow or deteriorate. These are permanent books.

Norbert Davis. There have been a lot of dogs in mystery fiction, from Baynard Kendrick's guide dog to Virginia Lanier's bloodhounds, but there's never been one quite like Carstairs. Doan, a short, chubby Los Angeles private eye, won Carstairs in a crap game, but there never is any question as to who the boss is in this relationship. Carstairs isn't just any Great Dane. He is so big that Doan figures he really ought to be considered another species. He scorns baby talk and belly rubs—unless administered by a pretty girl—and growls whenever Doan has a drink. His full name is Dougal's Laird Carstairs and as a sleuth he rarely barks up the wrong tree. He's down in Mexico with Doan, ostensibly to convince a missing fugitive that he would do well to stay put. The case is complicated by three murders, assorted villains, and a horrific earthquake that cuts the mountainous little village of Los Altos off from the rest of Mexico. Doan and Carstairs aren't the only unusual visitors to Los Altos. There's Patricia Van Osdel, a ravishing blonde whose father made millions from flypaper, and Captain Emile Perona, a Mexican policeman whose long-ago Spanish ancestor helped establish Los Altos. It's that ancestor who brings teacher Janet Martin to Mexico along with a stolen book that may contain the key to a secret hidden for hundreds of years in the village church. Written in the snappy hardboiled style of the day, *The Mouse in the Mountain* (0-915230-41-0, 151 pages, $14.00) was first published in 1943 and followed by two other Doan and Carstairs novels. "Each of these is fast-paced, occasionally lyrical in a hard-edged way, and often quite funny. Davis, in fact, was one of the few writers to successfully blend the so-called hardboiled story with farcical humor."—Bill Pronzini, *1001 Midnights.* Staff pick at The Sleuth of Baker Street in Toronto, Poisoned Pen in Scottsdale, Az., and Murder by the Book in Houston. Four star review in *Romantic Times.* "A laugh a minute romp...hilarious dialogue and descriptions...utterly engaging, downright fun read…fetch this one! Highly recommended."—Michelle A. Reed, *I Love a Mystery*. "Deft, charming…unique…one of my top ten all time favorite novels." Ed Gorman, *Mystery Scene*. "Sometimes when you've heard for years that a certain book is a cult classic or a past writer an undervalued master, it's hard for the reality to live up to the hype. Such is not the case with Norbert Davis's 1943 novel, *The Mouse in the Mountain*, the first of three novels about the team of Doan and Carstairs. The humor, the pace, the background of World War II-era Mexico, the surprising plot, and one of the great crime-fiction earthquakes combine to ratify the high opinion of pulp historians have of Davis, a gifted but tragic figure as shown in Tom and Enid Schantz's introduction. Doan is a deceptively ordinary-looking private eye with a distinctive style, and the Great Dane Carstairs is one of the most memorable animal characters in mystery fiction, his superior attitude and abilities made quite believable without undermining his essential canine nature."—Jon L. Breen, *Ellery Queen's Mystery Magazine*.

Joanna Cannan. The books by this English writer are among our most popular titles. Modern reviewers favorably compared our two Cannan reprints with the best books of the Golden Age of detective fiction. "Worthy of being discussed in the same breath with an Agatha Christie or a Josephine Tey."— Sally Fellows, Mystery News. "First-rate Golden Age detection with a likeable detective, a complex and believable murderer, and a level of style and craft that bears comparison with Sayers, Allingham, and Marsh."—Jon L. Breen, *Ellery Queen's Mystery Magazine*. Set in the late 1930s in a village that was a fictionalized version of Oxfordshire, both titles feature young Scotland Yard inspector Guy Northeast. *They Rang Up the Police* (0-915230-27-5, 156 pages, $14.00) and *Death at The Dog* (0-915230-23-2, 156 pages, $14.00).

Glyn Carr. The author is really Showell Styles, one of the foremost English mountain climbers of his era as well as one of that sport's most celebrated historians. Carr turned to crime fiction when he realized that mountains provided a ideal setting for committing murders. The 15 books featuring Shakespearean actor Abercrombie "Filthy" Lewker are set on peaks scattered around the globe, although the author returned again and again to his favorite climbs in Wales, where his first mystery, published in 1951, *Death on Milestone Buttress* (0-915230-29-1, 187 pages, $14.00), is set. Lewker is a marvelous Falstaffian character whose exploits have been praised by such discerning critics as Jacques Barzun and Wendell Hertig Taylor in *A Catalogue of Crime*. Other critics have been just as kind: "You'll get a taste of the Welsh countryside, will encounter names replete with consonants, will be exposed to numerous snippets from Shakespeare and will find Carr's novel a worthy representative of the cozies of two generations ago."—*I Love a Mystery.*

Clyde B. Clason. Clason has been praised not only for his elaborate plots and skillful use of the locked room gambit but also for his scholarship. He may be one of the few mystery authors—and no doubt the first—to provide a full bibliography of his sources. *The Man from Tibet* (0-915230-17-8, 220 pages, $14.00) is one of his best and highly recommended by the dean of locked room mystery scholars, Robert Adey, as "highly original." It's also one of the first popular novels to make use of Tibetan culture. Locked inside the Tibetan room of his Chicago apartment, the rich antiquarian was overheard repeating a forbidden occult chant under the watchful eyes of Buddhist gods. When the doors were opened, it appeared that he had succumbed to a heart attack. But the elderly Roman historian and sometime amateur sleuth Theocritus Lucius Westborough is convinced that Adam Merriweather's death was anything but natural and that the weapon was an eight century Tibetan manuscript.

Joan Coggin. *Who Killed the Curate?* Meet Lady Lupin Lorrimer Hastings, the young, lovely, scatterbrained and kindhearted newlywed wife to the vicar of St. Marks Parish in Glanville, Sussex. When it comes to matters clerical, she literally doesn't know Jews from Jesuits and she's hopelessly at sea at the meetings of the Mothers' Union, Girl Guides, or Temperance Society but she's determined to make husband Andrew proud of her—or, at least, not to embarrass him too badly. So when Andrew's curate is poisoned, Lady Lupin enlists the help of her old society pals, Duds and Tommy Lethbridge, as well as Andrew's nephew, a British secret service agent, to get at the truth. Lupin refuses to believe Diane Lloyd, the 38-year-old author of children's and detective stories could have done the deed, and casts her net out over the other parishioners. All the suspects seem so nice, much more so than the victim, and Lupin announces she'll help the killer escape if only he or she confesses. Imagine Gracie Allen of Burns and Allen or Pauline Collins of *No, Honestly* as a sleuth and you might get a tiny idea of what Lupin is like. Set at Christmas 1937 and first published in England in 1944, this is the first American appearance of *Who Killed the Curate?* "Coggin writes in the spirit of Nancy Mitford and E.M. Delafield. But the books are mysteries, so that makes them perfect."—Katherine Hall Page. "Marvelous."—*Deadly Pleasures.* (0-915230-44-5, $14.00).

Manning Coles. The two English writers who collaborated as Coles are best known for those witty spy novels featuring Tommy Hambledon, but they also wrote four delightful—and funny—ghost novels. *The Far Traveller* (0-915230-35-6, 154 pages, $14.00) is a stand-alone novel in which a film company unknowingly hires the ghost of a long-dead German graf to play himself in a movie. "I laughed until I hurt. I liked it so much, I went back to page 1 and read it a second time."—Peggy Itzen, *Cozies, Capers & Crimes*. The other three books feature two cousins, one English, one American, and their spectral pet monkey who got a little drunk and tried to stop—futilely and fatally—a German advance outside a small French village during the 1870 Franco-Prussian War. Flash forward to the 1950s where this comic trio of friendly ghosts rematerialize to aid relatives in danger in *Brief Candles* (0-915230-24-0, 156 pages, $14.00), *Happy Returns* (0-915230-31-3, 156 pages, $14.00) and *Come and Go* (0-915230-34-8, 155 pages, $14.00).

Elizabeth Dean. Dean wrote only three mysteries, but in Emma Marsh she created one of the first independent female sleuths in the genre. Written in the screwball style of the 1930s, *Murder is a Collector's Item* (0-915230-19-4, $14.00) is described in a review in *Deadly Pleasures* by award-winning mystery writer Sujata Massey as a story that "froths over with the same effervescent humor as the best Hepburn-Grant films." Like the second book in the trilogy, *Murder is a Serious Business* (0-915230-28-3, 254 pages, $14.95), it's set in a Boston antique store just as the Great Depression is drawing to a close. *Murder a Mile High* (0-915230-39-9, 188 pages, $14.00), moves to the Central City Opera House in the Colorado mountains, where Emma has been summoned by am old chum, the opera's reigning diva. Emma not only has to find a murderer, she may also have to catch a Nazi spy. A reviewer for a Central City area newspaper warmly greeted this reprint: "An endearing glimpse of Central City and Denver during World War II. . . . the dialogue twists and turns. . . . reads like a Nick and Nora movie. . . . charming."—*The Mountain-Ear*. "Fascinating."—*Romantic Times*.

Constance & Gwenyth Little. These two Australian-born sisters from New Jersey have developed almost a cult following among mystery readers. Critic Diane Plumley, writing in *Dastardly Deeds*, called their 21 mysteries "celluloid comedy written on paper." Each book, published between 1938 and 1953, was a stand-alone, but there was no mistaking a Little heroine. She hated housework, wasn't averse to a little gold-digging (so long as she called the shots), and couldn't help antagonizing cops and potential beaux. The Rue Morgue Press intends to reprint all of their books. Currently available: *The Black Coat* (0-915230-40-2, 155 pages, $14.00), *Black Corridors* (0-915230-33-X, 155 pages, $14.00), *The Black Gloves* (0-915230-20-8, 185 pages, $14.00), *Black-Headed Pins* (0-915230-25-9, 155 pages, $14.00), *The Black Honeymoon* (0-915230-21-6, 187 pages, $14.00), *The Black Paw* (0-915230-37-2, 156 pages, $14.00), *The Black Stocking* (0-915230-30-5, 154 pages, $14.00), *Great Black Kanba* (0-915230-22-4, 156 pages, $14.00), *The Grey*

Mist Murders (0-915230-26-7, 153 pages, $14.00), and *The Black Eye* (0-915230-45-3, 154 pages, $14.00).

Marlys Millhiser. Our only non-vintage mystery, *The Mirror* (0-915230-15-1, 303 pages, $17.95) is our all-time bestselling book, now in a sixth printing. How could you not be intrigued by a novel in which "you find the main character marrying her own grandfather and giving birth to her own mother," as one reviewer put it of this supernatural, time-travel (sort-of) piece of wonderful make-believe set both in the mountains above Boulder, Colorado, at the turn of the century and in the city itself in 1978. Internet book services list scores of rave reviews from readers who often call it the "best book I've ever read."

James Norman. The marvelously titled *Murder, Chop Chop* (0-915230-16-X, 189 pages, $13.00) is a wonderful example of the eccentric detective novel. "The book has the butter-wouldn't-melt-in-his-mouth cool of Rick in *Casablanca*."—*The Rocky Mountain News*. "Amuses the reader no end."—*Mystery News*. "This long out-of-print masterpiece is intricately plotted, full of eccentric characters and very humorous indeed. Highly recommended."—*Mysteries by Mail*. Meet Gimiendo Hernandez Quinto, a gigantic Mexican who once rode with Pancho Villa and who now trains *guerrilleros* for the Nationalist Chinese government when he isn't solving murders. At his side is a beautiful Eurasian known as Mountain of Virtue, a woman as dangerous to men as she is irresistible. Together they look into the murder of Abe Harrow, an ambulance driver who appears to have died at three different times. First published in 1942.

Sheila Pim. *Ellery Queen's Mystery Magazine* said of these wonderful Irish village mysteries that Pim "depicts with style and humor everyday life." *Booklist* said they were in "the best tradition of Agatha Christie." *Common or Garden Crime* (0-915230-36-4, 157 pages, $14.00) is set in neutral Ireland during World War II when Lucy Bex must use her knowledge of gardening to keep the wrong person from going to the gallows. Beekeeper Edward Gildea uses his knowledge of bees and plants to do the same thing in *A Hive of Suspects* (0-915230-38-0, 155 pages, $14.00). *Creeping Venom* (0-915230-42-9, 155 pages, $14.00) mixes politics and religion into a deadly mixture.

Charlotte Murray Russell. Spinster sleuth Jane Amanda Edwards tangles with a murderer and Nazi spies in *The Message of the Mute Dog* (0-915230-43-7, 156 pages, $14.00), a culinary cozy set just before Pearl Harbor. Jane Amanda ran roughshod over friends and relatives in twelve books. Our earlier title, *Cook Up a Crime*, is currently out of print.

Juanita Sheridan. Sheridan was one of the most colorful figures in the history of detective fiction, as you can see from Tom and Enid Schantz's introduction to *The Chinese Chop* (0-915230-32-1, 155 pages, $14.00). Her books are equally colorful, as well as showing how mysteries with female protagonists began changing after World War II. The postwar housing crunch finds Janice Cameron, newly arrived in New York City from Hawaii, without a place to live until she answers an ad for a roommate. It turns out the advertiser is an acquaintance from Hawaii, Lily Wu, whom critic Anthony Boucher (for whom Bouchercon, the World Mystery Convention, is named) described as an "exquisitely blended product of Eastern and Western cultures" and the only female sleuth that he "was devotedly in love with," citing "that odd mixture of respect for her professional skills and delight in her personal charms." First published in 1949, this ground-breaking book was the first of four to feature Lily and be told by her Watson, Janice, a first-time novelist. No sooner do Lily and Janice move into a rooming house in Washington Square than a corpse is found in the basement. In Lily Wu, Sheridan created one of the most believable—and memorable—female sleuths of her day. "Highly recommended."—*I Love a Mystery.* "This well-written. . .enjoyable variant of the boarding house whodunit and a vivid portrait of the post WWII New York City housing shortage, puts to lie the common misconception that strong, self-reliant, non-spinster-or-comic sleuths didn't appear on the scene until the 1970s. Chinese-American Lily Wu and her novelist Watson, Janice Cameron, are young and feminine but not dependent on men."—*Ellery Queen's Mystery Magazine.* Look for more books in this series in 2002.